The Estate

by

David McCormac

Contents

The New Girl

Characters

Tracey

A black woman in her mid forties. She is the main character in the book. She has two children and a husband in name only.

Sally

An attractive woman in her late thirties. She is of medium height and has a slim attractive figure. Sally is a single woman, who has a fifteen year-old daughter. She spent time in jail after stabbing her ex-husband in the back.

Bone Crusher Bet

A large lesbian woman who you wouldn't want to get on the wrong side of. She is in her fifties and small in height. She is all muscle and very loyal to her friends. She has twin boys who are nearly sixteen.

Halima

An Asian woman who is single and lives with her mother. She is in her forties. Her mother is a great cook, which shows on Halima's waist line.

Sandra

A tall woman in her mid forties, although she looks ten years younger. She takes care of her body and appearance due to her high sexual appetite. She enjoys playing famous characters in her sexual role play.

Pop it in Pat

A small average size woman in her early sixties. She is married with eight children and fifteen grand children.

Miss Spears

A woman in her early sixties. She is the supervisor who is a strict disciplinarian, especially when people are not pulling their weight.

Adrian Acne

A tall man in his mid thirties. He has a face full of spots which is putting a strain on their marriage.

Maxi Bates

A young lad of nineteen who keeps getting erections hence the reason he is always putting his hands in his pockets.

Mandy Minger

A small woman in her early thirties. She has a major problem with her hygiene, hence everyone keeps their distance.

Setting

A garment making factory in the middle of a council estate.

The New Girl

Tracey walks into the factory and after clocking on, she walks over to her sewing machine.

Halima
Morning love.

Bet
You been on the drink again?

Tracey
I wish I bloody had.

Pat
Don't tell us you have let your Reggie share your bed again?

Tracey
With two kids already, what do you think?

Bet
So why the late arrival?

Tracey
Crazy Chris at 105, I've had flashing blue lights through my bedroom window for much of the night.

Halima
What's her problem this time?

Tracey
She keeps dialling 999 and asking for an ambulance as her baby is on the way, I wouldn't mind so much, but she was seventy-five last year. She walks around with a mini skirt on and no teeth in her

mouth. She hasn't been with a man for years. The only dark passage she should be filling is a dark passage on the way to a padded cell. *(They all laugh)*

Sandra
Watch out. Spearsey is on her way.

The shop floor supervisor walks over to Tracey's machine. She has Sally with her.

Miss Spears
It's nice of you to join us Mrs Green. It seems your workplace is just an afterthought these days.

Bet
Tracey, keep your mouth shut.

Miss Spears
It's not her mouth she needs to keep shut but her legs. How many kids have you got now?

Tracey
Just the two.

Miss Spears
More like two hundred.

Bet
No Tracey.

Miss Spears
This is Miss Docker who will be working alongside you. With Mrs Green's work ethic, she couldn't fill a person's shoes, never mind her boots. But with your surname being 'Docker', it will remind me how much money I need to dock from Mrs Green's pay this week.

Tracey stands up clenching her fists. Bet races over and gets hold of Tracey.

Bet
Leave it.

Miss Spear
(Walking away) You know where my office is if you want your P45.

Tracey
I'm going to smack that bitch.

Bet
Not in here you are not. Remember that you have got two kids and a useless husband to keep. *(Bet lets go and turns to Sally)* I'm Bet. Welcome to the family.

Sally
Does it always get as lively as this?

Bet
Love, strap yourself in and hold on tight, this place will give you the ride of your life and I don't mean from the blokes who work here. *(Bet goes and sits down in front of her machine).*

Tracey
Sorry about that. I'll get that bitch one day. So your name is Sally Docker then?

Sally
That's me, although I need to change my surname. It brings too many bad memories of my ex.

Tracey
A right pig was he?

Sally

You could say that because his last name was Docker, his preferred footwear was Docker boots, boots that regularly gave me a good kicking. I got to know many of the nurses by their first names.

Tracey

Did you not go to the police?

Sally

I did, but every time they wanted to prosecute him I backed down. He would get round me with flowers and promises of designer handbags. So when the police dropped the charges the devil would come out again and back to the gutter I would go. When he keeps telling you that you are trash and not fit to lick his boots, you start to believe it. So you think you deserve the beating he gives you everyday.

Tracey

How did you get it to stop?

Sally

After my usual kicking he turned his anger on my daughter. To hear your ten year old screaming, I snapped. I picked up the kitchen knife and thrusted it into his back. He fell to the floor and for a few seconds there was silence. I can now understand why they say silence is golden. At that moment, all my fears lifted out of me and whatever happened to me from that moment, I was free. I picked up my daughter and ran to my mothers. An hour later the police were knocking at the door. I got three years, but with good behaviour, I only did eighteen months.

Tracey

What happened to your daughter?

Sally

My mother got custody.

Tracey

How's your relationship with your mother now?

Sally

Non existent really. I see her once every couple of weeks when I go and pick up my daughter. That's all the courts would give me, my mother saw to that. But in fairness she did take on a traumatised ten year old, who I should never have been allowed to see and hear the things she did.

Tracey

What happened to your ex?

Sally

He is in a wheelchair, the knife went through his spine. He lives with a woman he was having an affair with behind my back. I hear she slaps him around a bit. What goes around comes around.

Tracey

Welcome to your new life. Let me fill you in on this shower who work here. You know the film the Dirty Dozen?

Sally

Yes, I watched it the other week.

Tracey

Well, here's the Dirty Dozen Part Two, the female revenge. You have met Bet, they call her 'Bone Crusher Bet.' As you can see, she is built like a brick shit house, so keep on her good side, that way you always got your back covered. She has twin boys.

Sally

I thought she was a lesbian?

Tracey

She is, but she went through a maternal period.

Sally

How did she get on with the penetration bit?

Tracey

That's the bit she was dreading, especially as her front bit had never been opened up to the light. But after a couple of months she felt she was ready to do 'the dirty deed' as she puts it. So at the beginning of February, on a bitterly cold night she headed to the White Heart pub with a couple of mates.

Sally

I remember that pub, if you were eighteen or over, you were considered to be geriatric and were expected to drink in the snug with the wrinklies.

Tracey

That's the one. Anyway they got a drink and sat down at the table. As Bet takes a sip of her pint, her eyes fell on a young blond guy who was sitting with some friends at the next table. She switched her radar tabs on and listened to his conversation.

Sally

What did she hear?

Tracey

She heard that he was a second year student at London University, he was studying English and History. His father worked for the government and his mother was a doctor. With his beautiful looks and athletic body, she knew there and then that her child had to possess his genes. To cut a long story short at the end of the night, the young guy found himself staggering along the street on his own. This gave Bet the green light. As she started to talk to him, she manoeuvred him to a wooded area where she quickly got his trousers and undies down. After being inside her for about ten minutes, he started to sober up, but with a vice like grip he had no chance to escape. It took another ten minutes for him to finish off. Releasing her grip, the guy pulled up his trousers and made a run for it. Bet slowly walked home, knowing that all her planning wasn't in vain.

Sally

Had it worked?

Tracey

Nine months later she gave birth to twin boys, who like their father, are blonde and academically gifted. Bet put their names down for Cambridge University. However there was one thing she didn't foresee.

Sally

What was that?

Tracey

One of the twins is gay, which looking back, Bet said the guy kept smiling when she grabbed his ass, in order to keep him upright.

Sally

Doesn't she worry that he will turn up on her door step one day?

Tracey

All the time. But the twins are sixteen next month, so there's not much time left for him to make a claim on them. Two rows down is 'Pop it in Pat.'

Sally

What does she pop in?

Tracey

Well, with eight kids, by four husbands, I'll let you figure that one out. I say Pat, how many grand kids do you have?

Pat

Fifteen. Thank goodness two of my own children are gay. If they were not, I would of hit the twenty mark. What with birthdays and

Christmas, it's the only reason I come to work. They cost me a bloody fortune. I nearly forgot *(shouting)* ladies stop your machines *(this they do)* my grand daughter, Kelly, got herself pregnant, so I'm going to be a great grandma.

Miss Spears
(Coming out of her office) What is going on here? Get back to your machines, we have an order to finish. That means you too Mrs Green.

Tracey
I say Sally, did you watch Chitty Chitty Bang Bang at the weekend. The child catcher always freaks me out.

Miss Spears
If he was looking to catch skivers then you would be in his cage, twenty four seven. Work Mrs Green. *(Miss Spears walks away)*

Tracey
Vile bitch.

Sally
No children then?

Tracey
No man to ever make them. Then you have got Halima who is a good friend to us all. She still lives at home with her mother, long story, but if you ever get invited round to eat, go, the food is amazing, as you can see by Halima's waist line. Next to her is Sandra.

Sally
She is very beautiful.

Tracey
She uses that beauty to play the leading lady in many of the famous films. She enjoys role play when it comes to meeting men for sexual pleasure. At the front you have got Lesley B, who is the union rep.

Sally

Has she had them enhanced?

Tracey

No every mile is natural. *(They both laugh)* With the dirty minded owner, they come very handy when she represents us workers.

Sally

Who's that sitting on her own?

Tracey

That's Mandy Minger.

Sally

Who is it?

Tracey

Mandy Minger. She lives on the other side of Mildenhall.

Sally

She looks a bit shabby.

Tracey

You might say shabby, but filthy and dirty are words that come to mind. Even the rats wipe their feet on the way out of her place. It was her birthday the other week, so we all clubbed together and brought her some perfume. It allowed us to go half a mile near her, as oppose to a mile.

Sally

No children then?

Tracey

No bloke can manage to get near her. Although saying that, one bloke did try with a mask on, but when she opened her front door, not even the gas mask could protect him. He collapsed on the ground and an ambulance had to be called. But despite her hygiene problems, she is a bloody good machinist. That's why management turns the other nose. *(They both laugh)* Looking at your sewing, you are not so bad yourself. That's a nice bit of sewing.

Sally

Thanks. Who is that over there? She seems to be swaying a bit.

Tracey

That's Gina Gin. Half her wages are spent on her gin habit. The trouble is though, now they have brought out all these different flavours she is lucky if she has got a tenner left by the end of the week. The woman next to her is Dirty Mouth Deb. The stuff that comes out of her mouth turns the air blue, but she is so funny. Also we must not forget our resident author, Davina Mack. She has two books published, with her third coming out soon.

Sally

I wondered why I kept seeing her writing.

Tracey

She went to a funeral the other week, and set up a stall next to the church door. If you have ever read one of her books, you would know that they are not the sort of books to sell at a funeral. Vibrators, front bottoms, penises and a woman with massive tits and that is in the first chapter. So while the mourners are sat there waiting for the coffin to arrive, they start reading Davina's book. Well, the church was in uproar with uncontrollable laughter. When the vicar invited people up to the pulpit to do a reading, Davina read a chapter from her new book. Even the widow couldn't contain herself. I said to her, "Don't you think that was a bit inappropriate?" she said "I made a hundred pounds that day, the most I've ever made at a funeral. While I think about it, there are a couple of lads to watch out for, when they bring over your material.

Sally

Is anyone normal in this place?

Tracey

If we were normal, no-one would be here. Now there is Adrian Acne, or as we like to say the AA man because his face keeps breaking out. So because of his spots, if he brings you any material watch out no puss gets on the fabric.

Sally

It's like a scene out of a horror movie.

Tracey

That sums his marriage up at the moment.

Sally

What's the problem?

Tracey

Well because of his fungal face, all their sexual activity occurs from behind, which as a woman she feels she is being short changed. She took an ad out in one of the magazines and it read "Front passengers to rent, no previous owners."

Sally

Has he not tried various things to get rid of them?

Tracey

He has tried everything, but not even the AA could get that face up and running.

Sally

Bless him.

Tracey

The other guy is Maxi Bates. He is the young guy you can see over there with his hands in his pockets.

Sally

What is he doing?

Tracey

Trying to extinguish life in his lower regions. His hands rarely see the light of day. Last year he went to Spain on holiday. He brought some swimming trunks and his mum had to stitch side pockets into them.

Sally

Bloody hell.

Tracey

Also watch out for Kain Cocaine. Dirty Mouth Deb found some white powder on some of the material she was working on. She sniffed it, thinking it was baby powder, five minutes later she was reciting the Lord's Prayers and singing 'All Things Bright and Beautiful.' We all called her Sister Mary Clarence for weeks after that.

Sandra

Guess who I bumped into the other day?

Bet

Who?

Sandra

Ethel.

Bet

How's she getting on?

Sandra

She is living life to the full. She was saying she has been to the east coast twice already this year.

Sally

Who was Ethel?

Tracey

She used to sit where you are sitting now. How long had she

been here?

Halima

It must have been over twenty years. She took me under her wing when I joined straight after leaving school, which was around ten years ago.

Sandra

So you are telling me you're twenty-six?

Bet

She is getting mixed up with her waist measurements.

Halima

You couple of witches.

Sandra

Well, I left school thirty years ago and you were a couple of years above me.

Halima

Well you would never guess that with my youthful looks.

Sandra

That's only be cause the lines and wrinkles have not got through the fat yet.

Halima

You nasty cow.

Tracey

Ladies.

Bet

Where?

Tracey

We were talking about how nice Ethel was.

Bet

She was nice. Always there for you if you had a problem.

Sandra

She would always cover for you. If you had to clock off a bit earlier because you were meeting a new bloke who you knew was loaded and would want to buy you a double gin and tonic, then you turned to Ethel.

Halima

So why did she leave?

Tracey

She had just turned sixty and got five numbers and the bonus on the lottery so she decided to retire early.

Bet

How much did she win?

Tracey

She never said, but it must have been more than a hundred thousand. We all went out the night she left to celebrate.

Halima

She brought us all of half a cider.

Bet

She did with all that money she had won.

Sandra

The tight bitch. I didn't know whether to drink it or throw it all over her.

Halima

Lets be honest, she only listened to our problems because she was a nosy cow.

Tracey

When she smiled you could see her rotten teeth, it put you off your dinner.

Bet

I'm glad she is gone, she always thought she was better than anyone else. No wonder her husband left her for a younger woman. He always said she was frigid.

Sally

Bloody hell, I should hate to think of someone who left who you didn't like. She would be picking knifes out of her back for weeks. *(They all laugh)*

Tracey

Have you seen the time? We should have clocked out five minutes ago.

They all switch off their machines and clock off. Outside the factory Bet, Sandra and Halima walk off down Beckhampton Road together, while Tracey and Sally walk up the hill. They stop at Tracey's gate.

Sally

The hill kills you.

Tracey

You get used to it. Number eighty, this is me. Do me a favour, Sally love, call for me in the morning. I couldn't afford to be late again with that bitch Spearsey on my back.

Sally

I'll give you a knock at seven.

Tracey

You are a star. I'll see you tomorrow.

Tracey walks up her path and Sally walks down the other side of the hill.

Workers 1, Management 0

Characters

Lesley Babbington

A Dolly Parton lookalike. She is in her early forties and is the trade union rep. She is having an affair with the boss.

Mr Thomas

Also in his mid forties, he is the owner of the factory. He is six feet tall, married and has three grown-up children.

Katrina

A small woman in her early seventies. Her life is devoted to her cats. She treats them all as her children.

Jay

He is fourteen, and Tracey's youngest child. He is not a popular child, due to the fact that he can't keep a secret.

Charlene

She is eighteen and Tracey's daughter. She is very attractive and popular with other people although she prefers to do as little as possible.

Brenda

A small dumpy woman, in her early sixties. She says it like it is. She has a criminal family, who are up to all sorts.

Mr Husain

A tall man in his late forties. He is the general manager of the factory.

Other characters

Tracey, Sandra, Bet, Halima and Mrs Spears.

Setting

The factory's shop floor.
The canteen of the factory.

Workers 1, Management 0

Sally walks up Tracey's path and knocks on her door. Jay, Tracey's son, opens the door.

Jay

My mum is a bit short this week, due to the fact she married the wrong man. Can she pay you next week, as she is going to trade him in for a younger model? *(Tracey comes to the door)*

Tracey

Morning Sally love, get yourself in here, the kettle has just boiled.

Sally

I see you have got him trained well, does it work?

Tracey

Usually, they feel sorry for him having two unfit parents. Here you go girl *(she hands Sally a mug of tea)* Right a quick fag then we are off. *(She opens her fag packet and sees it is half empty)* Who the bloody hell has been at my fags?

Jay

Well, I did see Charlene in the garden with her boyfriend yesterday. They both looked like dragons with smoke coming out of their mouths whilst they were kissing.

Tracey

Thank you for your honesty Jay, but you do know, you will never be a popular boy. It's time for me to slay the dragon. *(Shouting from the bottom of the stairs)* Charlene!

Charlene

(Who is in bed) What?

Tracey

Why are half of my fags missing?

Charlene

Don't blame me, I don't even smoke.

Tracey

There better be twenty fags on that kitchen table when I get home. If there is not your behind will be smoking. Talking of dragons, George *(Tracey's husband)* get yourself out of your pit and get this place cleaned up. Remember I'm the only dragon who wins the battles around here. *(She walks back into the kitchen)* You see Jay, your sister might be a lying, two faced waste of space, but she will always be popular with many friends. Right, come on Sally love, I can't be late again.

They both hurry out of the house and start walking down the hill.

Sally

Looking at peoples gardens, it always surprises me how some people look after their front gardens and others couldn't give a toss. I mean, look at this garden. How many weeds can you pack into a small space?

Tracey

That Peg Leg Pat's place. She is a lady of the night, so being on nights, doesn't give her much time for gardening. She advertises herself on social media as a leggy blonde who will kick you into touch. She plays a striker who always puts the balls in the back of the net. It's a bit like football meets polo. But when it's not match day, she just throws her false leg over her back and gets on with it.

Sally

Here we all are. I can't believe we are two minutes early. I don't know how you are going to cope.

Tracey

Bitch. *(They both laugh)*

Bet

Morning ladies.

Tracey

Morning Bet.

Miss Spears

(Walking over) Two minute early Miss Green, did you piss the bed?

Tracey

I wish you would piss off.

Miss Spears

Using bad language to your supervisor are we? You better have a chat with your trade union rep, you're going to need her. *(She walks away)*

Tracey

That's what you get for being on time.

Sandra

That's what you get when you open your gob.

Tracey

Well, she winds me up.

Lesley B

(Lesley B walks over) You have got a disciplinary meeting this afternoon Tracey love, we will have a chat at lunch time. I'll come and find you. *(She walks away)*

Tracey

Could my day get any worse?

Halima

It's not even eight o'clock yet.

Tracey

What are we machining today?

Bet

We have just got an order in to make a thousand mini skirts.

Pat

Apparently they are back in fashion.

Sandra

Looking at Mandy Minger's legs, any skirts would look like a mini skirt on her.

Halima

How do you get legs that big?

Tracey

Sitting on your lard rear, stuffing your mouth as you are watching television until two o'clock in the morning.

Sandra

Do you remember wearing a mini Bet?

Bet

You taking the piss? I rip them off, not put them on.

Sandra

How is your sex life going?

Bet

I had to let one go the other day.

Sandra

Why was that?

Bet

You know when you have been to the toilet and after you take a piece of toilet paper to dab your private place?

Tracey

Private place, that's the first time I've heard you call it that.

Bet

You would, because most woman around here don't keep it private, because theirs is always on show. Anyway, before I was rudely interrupted, rather than use toilet paper she used the bath towel, which although I didn't have a problem with it, Anthony...

Tracey

(To Sally) That's Bet's gay son.

Bet

...complained about the towel smelling of fish when he used it after for a shower.

Halima

He's got a point.

Bet

But what was more shocking is that she never put the toilet seat down.

Tracey

That's disgusting.

Sandra

For a woman to not put down the toilet seat is shocking.

Halima

It's one of the vilest things I've ever heard of.

Tracey

No wonder you got rid. Filthy bitch. Bloody hell it's nearly lunch time. I think I'll have a salad with a bowl of chips.

Sandra

That's very healthy. Tracey love, what's brought this on?

Tracey

It's doing these mini skirts. With summer just around the corner, I want to show off my slim figure to the world. What are you having Halima?

Halima

I was going to have chips, pie and peas.

Tracey

You're not planning on wearing a mini skirt any time soon then?

Halima

I could wear a mini skirt everyday of the week.

Bet

I didn't know Evans stocked them?

Halima

What's that supposed to mean?

Tracey

I mean, next summer, will be the time for you to shine.

As Tracey finished talking, the doors fling open and a woman dressed in black collapses on the floor. She begins to cry out loud.

Bet

Here we go again.

Tracey
Another one must have died.

Lesley B walks over to console her.

Sally
What's going on?

Tracey
It's Katrina the cat woman. Her cats are her life, so much so she is still working in her seventies.

Lesley B
Tracey love, take her to the canteen and try and calm her down. I'll have a word with management to see if she can go home.

Tracey leads Katrina up to the canteen. They both sit down.

Tracey
Brenda *(who is in charge of the canteen)* get us a couple of teas love.

Brenda
OK pet. *(Tracey rolls her eyes)*

Katrina
Why does it have to happen to me. He was my baby, my child, and now he has gone.

Tracey
What happened love?

Katrina
I was just sweeping the path as the milk float pulled up outside the flats, on the other side of the road. I could see that Miss Lowe was having her usual two pints, as was Mrs Goodwin. Although I did think it was a bit odd that Mrs Humphrey's was only having the one pint with

Nelly Greenwood not having any at all. She always has at least one pint a day. As the milk man got back into his milk float I saw my Sooty go underneath the float. I shouted at him to come away but it was too late, because as he drove away my child got caught underneath the wheels. He bolted out and a few yards along the road he collapsed. I ran out of the gate and picked him up but he was gone Tracey. I collapsed to my knees and through my tears I just kept saying 'why, why' Sheila Pickering came running out to help me, but with the state of her net curtains and a front step that has never seen a scrubbing brush. I thanked her for helping me, but made a quick exit, so that none of the neighbours could see who I was associating with. Luckily, Janet Henry came round, she keeps her house and garden very tidy.

Tracey

How old was he?

Katrina

He had just turned three.

Tracey

What colour was he?

Katrina

He was pure white when he came into my life and stayed that way for the first year.

Tracey

Why just the first year?

Katrina

Well, I brought some new curtains, which were green and try as I may, my Sooty just didn't look right next to them. So as they were two hundred pounds a pair, and that was in the sales, I dyed the cat the same colour as the curtains. After that he would never do as he was told. He would come in late at night and I would say to him 'What time do you call this? You know you are not old enough to be out this late.' I even told him that while you are living under my roof, you will stick to my rules. He weed all over my kitchen floor in defiance. He kept turning his nose up at his food. I brought him tins of salmon and tuna and even cooked him fresh fish. He still wasn't happy. Even when he got next doors cat pregnant, I stuck up for him and told them that he was gay. What more could I have done for my beautiful child? *(She begins to cry loudly again)*

Tracey

You are a wonderful mother.

Katrina

I must go home and mourn for my boy. *(She pulls out a black veil from her bag and walks out of the canteen with the veil over her face)*

Lesley B

(Walking into the canteen)

Tracey

Just gone.

Lesley B

Well we won't see her now, until after the funeral. Right then, I've heard you've been telling The Wicked Witch of the West to piss off.

Tracey

She winds me up something rotten. I was two minutes early clocking on and she asks me if I had pissed the bed.

Lesley B

She said that to you, did she?

Tracey

She did.

Lesley B

If that's the case, you having nothing to worry about, leave everything to me. When I give you the wink bring on the tears, you are going to see one of my Oscar winning performances. I think the white bra with two buttons open will do the trick. I'll come for you at two, see you in a bit love. *(She walks away)*

Sally, Bet, Halima and Sandra walk through the canteen doors.

Bet

Here she is Mother Teresa.

Halima

She has the Samaritans written all over her. I'm bloody starving. *(They all rush over to the queue)*

Brenda

Chips, pie and peas Bet?

Bet

No I fancy a salad.

Brenda

Did I hear your right? You said a salad?

Everyone in the queue turns around and tells the next person that Bet is having a salad. This spreads to the whole of the canteen. There is two minutes of silence. After which everyone goes back to what they were doing.

Bet

Yes Brenda. I thought with the summer around the corner, I could do with losing a few pounds.

Brenda

It's your choice, but I'll put a pie to one side, just in case.

Bet

Thank you Brenda. *(Bet pays for her meal and goes to sit down)*

Brenda

Now then our Tracey, what can I do you for?

Tracey

Just a salad with a bowl of chips.

Brenda

Bloody hell, have you all joined Weight Watchers.

Tracey

It's Chinese night tonight so I've got to leave some room.

Brenda

Don't make a habit of it. *(Looking at Sally)* Now what can I get for you young lady?

Tracey

This is Sally Bren, she is our newest family member.

Brenda

Hello Sally love.

Sally

Hello, just a cheese sandwich for me.

Brenda

Someone else who has joined Weight Watchers. I'll have to put a sign up saying this way to the healthy cafe. Don't tell me you have joined Weight Watchers too Halima?

Halima

Does sausage, chips and beans sound healthy to you?

Brenda

Now there's a girl who knows what's good for her.

Halima

I do, that's why I have stayed the same weight for years.

Sandra

So your Sari's have always struggled to cover you.

Halima

Carry on and you will be wearing sausage, chips and beans.

Bet

(Shouting from her table) You two, shut it. We have already got one member of the family in the dog house. *(Tracey starts to bark. Everyone laughs)*

Tracey

Talking about the dog house, you are looking a bit rough our Bet, everything alright?

Bet

(After a few seconds of silence) Yeah, I'm fine. I think I have a bit of a cold coming on.

Tracey

If you are sure.

Sally

I say, that Brenda tells it like it is.

Tracey

She don't mix her words that one. If you need anything and I mean anything, then Brenda's the woman to go to. If she can't get it, her three grown-up sons can.

Bet

Isn't her Craig still inside?

Tracey

No, he came out last month. They let him out six months earlier for good behaviour which is a bit of a joke seeing that he made more money on the inside in a year than he's made on the outside. So Sally love, if you need any type of drugs, Craig's your man. If you need a bit of company of an evening, Brenda's second son Mark can sort that out for you. He does a bit of sex trafficking on the side. Brenda's youngest son is a cat burglar, so if you need anything for the home or yourself, he will sort it out for you.

Sally

They seem to have everything covered.

Tracey

Doits by name, do it by nature. Without them, I wouldn't have been able to get half of the stuff for my place.

Bet

I'll give them his due, he always gets quality stuff. I've had my fridge freezer for years and it still works like new.

Tracey

That's like my cooker. Just write down the size and make and it will be with you the next day.

Brenda

All three of them give excellent service. Nothing is too much trouble for them.

Halima

(Sitting down) I'm sure she has put up her prices.

Tracey

She will have, it's getting near the holiday season. I bet she is off to Ibiza again.

Sally

She looks a bit old to go clubbing.

Tracey

She doesn't go for the clubs but more for the sex.

Sally

Really?

Tracey

She always stays next to the eighteen to thirties resort. So comes the end of the night, when all the young ones are pissed and coming out of the clubs, she pounces. Let's be honest, when you are pissed and every single girl looks like a princess, she prides herself on getting off with a guy every night.

Sally

How long does she go for?

Tracey

Usually fourteen nights.

Sally

That's fourteen blokes.

Tracey

As she says, a princess needs to kiss a few frogs before she gets to her prince.

Bet

Right come on you lot, it's time we were getting back.

They all stack up their plates and head down to the shop floor.

They sit behind their machines and start work. An hour later, Lesley B walks over to Tracey.

Lesley B

We will be ready for you in about ten minutes, just time for you to go to the toilet and have a quick fag.

Tracey goes to the toilet and afterwards she has a quick fag. Then she walks to Mr Thomas's office, where as she walks through his door, she can see Mr Thomas, Mr Hussain and Miss Spears all sitting along the back wall. There are two chairs facing them. Lesley B is sitting on one of them and Tracey goes to sit on the other one.

Mr Thomas

Now that you are here, I understand that you swore at my supervisor telling her to piss off?

Just as Tracey is going to speak, Lesley B puts her hand on Tracey's arm to stop her from answering the question. She winks at Tracey, which gives Tracey the queue to cry.

Lesley B

As you can see Mrs Green is still in shock by the whole episode. She is not denying the fact that she said what she did, but it was a response. To the comments that Miss Spears had made a few seconds earlier. *(She undoes another button on her blouse which both Mr Thomas and Mrs Hussain find themselves staring at)*

Mr Thomas

(Stuttering) I'm not aware of this. Please do enlighten us.

Lesley B

(Lesley drops her pen and as she picks it up, she reveals more of her cleavage) Mrs Green arrived two minutes early to start her shift. Having clocked on, Miss Spears was heard to say and I quote "I see you are two minutes early Mrs Green, did you piss the bed?"

Miss Spears

I only said it in fun.

Lesley B

Fun to who Miss Spears? It certainly wasn't fun for Mrs Green, due to her medical conditions.

Mr Thomas

What medical conditions are those?

Lesley B

Vaginal yeast infection. Along with incontinence, this not only see's Mrs Green's vagina becoming inflamed when her overheated urine passes through but with her incontinence there are times when her water comes out in a raging torrent, enough to fill two full sized Olympic swimming pools.

Mr Thomas

Did you know about this Miss Spears?

Miss Spears

I didn't Mr Thomas.

Lesley B

The reason for this is obvious, Mrs Green felt she was unable to approach Miss Spears about such a private matter. Surely Mr Thomas, your managerial staff have been trained to help with the well being of the workers. Leaving that door open if any workers would wish to confide with any problems they may have, Let's face it Mr Thomas, I know your door is always open to me, if I need to get something off my chest.

Mr Thomas

(Stuttering) Thank you Miss Babbington. I have taken on board what you have said and due to this new evidence *(looking at Miss Spears)* that I was not aware of, you are free to go Mrs Green.

Lesley B

And Mr Thomas will it be alright if Mrs Green can go to the toilet when she needs to? We don't want to be swimming for our lives do we?

Mr Thomas

That will be fine Miss Babbington.

Tracey and Lesley B leave Mr Thomas's office and walks along the shop floor.

Tracey

Thank you Lesley love, you were bloody amazing.

Lesley B

All in a day's work my love. It's half past three, so get yourself clocked off and have a good weekend.

Tracey

You too love.

Tracey gives Lesley a big hug, then goes to clock off and is seen walking out the door.

New Beginnings

Characters

Barbra Light

A small woman in her mid forties. She is married with one son. She is a very good neighbour to Tracey as she is very reliable and honest.

Joan

A tall woman in her late thirties. She is married with two children. She likes a good gossip and like Barbra she can be relied upon if you need a favour.

Doreen

A small woman in her late sixties. She has lived on the estate all her life and is the mother of Tracey. Despite her age, she acts and looks like someone half her age.

Malcolm

A tall business man in his forties. He is a wealthy man who lives on the posh side of town. He is very happy to talk about his wealth in his quest to look down on people.

Caroline

A slender woman in her mid thirties. Like her husband, she is very happy to show off her wealth. Her status and position in society is the most important thing to her, with love taking a low third.

George

A small man in his mid fifties. He is the husband of Tracey. He does not work as for the last few years he has suffered from depression and anxiety which allows him to do very little.

Other characters
Tracey and Jay.

Setting
Tracey's house and garden.

New Beginnings

Tracey is taking the washing out of the washing machine and putting it in the basket. She then goes out into the garden to put the washing on the line.

Barbra

(Hanging out her washing) Morning Tracey.

Tracey

Morning Barbra. I thought your washing day was Monday?

Barbra

It is usually, but I've got to go and have my bunions done so I will be staying in hospital over night. I wouldn't have bothered but my Raymond had always had a foot fetish and its painful when he starts sucking my toes.

Tracey

He always did like it when you put your foot in it. *(They both laugh)*

Joan

Hello Barbra, hello Tracey.

Tracey/Barbra

Morning Joan.

Joan

It looks like we all had the same idea this morning.

Tracey

You usually do your washing mid week.

Joan

I do, but our Richard is not well.

Tracey

Nothing serious I hope?

Joan

Diarrhoea, he had an accident in the night. I've boiled his bedding twice but there's still a brown tint, but it's clean.

Barbra

It reminds you when they were babies and you spent hours boiling their nappies, you never got them fully clean either.

Tracey

But we always put them back on, stains or no stains.

Joan

You had too, money was tight.

Barbra

You never saw a pair of jeans without patches in.

Tracey

Mend and make do. These younguns don't know their born today.

Joan

Have you heard?

Barbra

What?

Joan

Jane with the eyes has died.

Tracey

She's not.

Joan

Well I was on the bus and who should get on but Mrs Bloomer.

Barbra

Don't tell me, she talked about all her personal life and then when she was getting off the bus she tells you to not say anything and to keep it a secret.

Joan

She did.

Barbra

She said the same to me last Friday.

Tracey

And to me the Friday before that.

Joan

Anyway, sitting there in her cheese cloth dress.

Barbra

That dress has always been an old favourite of hers.

Tracey

She was still wearing that dress when the Romans invaded.

Joan

She told me that Jane with the eyes had just walked up the garden path to dig some potatoes up for their tea. She was going to make a meat and potato pie, when all of a sudden she fell to the floor with a heart attack.

Barbra

Did it kill her straight away?

Joan

No, not straight away. She lost the use of her speech and arms, but her legs were still working, so for an hour she had to signal to someone using her legs like frogs do. But nobody came, until her creepy son Vain Vinnie saw her through the window. He had been looking through the window for a bit, you know how dirty her windows were.

Barbra

They were shocking.

Joan

Windolene was a swear word in their house. In fact, the window would have been cleaner if the house had stood in the middle of Trafalgar Square. Well he rushes outside and seeing that his mother was still alive, he ran to the phone for an ambulance. Now as you know, the hall mirror is on the wall directly behind the phone. As he was dialling 999, Vain Vinnie looked into the mirror and saw that he had a couple of hairs out of place which made him feel ill, so much so that he rushed to the bathroom and spent the next half a hour sorting his hair out.

Barbra

Half a hour?

Joan

Yeah. He had to wash it, dry it and apply a load more mousse to it. Then he remembered his mother was near to death, so he raced down stairs and phoned for an ambulance. It only took the ambulance fifteen minutes to get there, half the time that it had took to do his hair.

Tracey

Did they get to her in time?

Joan

She died five minutes before they arrived.

Barbra

Hair today, gone tomorrow.

Tracey

I bet Vain Vinnie was devastated?

Joan

He said he would have been if his hair had not looked right when the ambulance crew had arrived.

Barbra

Shocking. It is just as bad as her oldest son buying a new Jaguar but he couldn't afford to run it, so it stood outside the house for the next two years. Do you know he has never done a day's work in his life?

Joan

Her husband wasn't much better. Remember when he ran off with that woman half his age? She helped him run up thousands for pounds in debt and when he couldn't get any more credit she dumped him.

Barbra

She did. I'm surprised Jane with the eyes had him back.

Tracey

So am I. But they never slept in the same bed again.

Barbra

When is the funeral?

Joan

It was last week.

Tracey

I would have gone if I had known.

Barbra

Was there a wake?

Joan

Not as such. They did invite people to the pub, but you had to by your own drink and there was no food.

Barbra
No food, I'm glad I didn't go.

Joan
Well with one son spreading half his money on grooming products and the other unable to run his car there wasn't much hope of getting anything to eat.

Barbra
You have to keep your standards up in both life and death.

Peter Pan the ice cream van comes down the road, ringing his bell.

Tracey
I don't know how he has the nerve. I've stopped my Jay from going to him.

Joan
What's he done?

Tracey
He was taking young girls around with him in his van.

Joan
That's terrible.

Tracey
Apparently he covered his private parts with ice cream and afterwards he put a flake in it and covered it in sprinkles. Then he started to sing "There is only one cornetto, give it to me!"

Barbra
He should be locked up.

Tracey
Well one of the girls complained to her mother. The next minute

the police were at his door. He has been bailed until his court appearance next month. Our Jay has made up a song about him.

Joan

Go on Tracey love, give us a song.

Tracey

(Singing)
Peter Pan, is a dirty old man,
Peter Pan takes girls in his van,
Peter Pan will rob you if he can,
Peter Pan is a filthy ice cream man.

Barbra

(Clapping) That was amazing.

Joan

Well, I'll definitely keep my two away from him.

Barbra

Did you hear about the other night?

Tracey

No. What happened?

Barbra

Well our Jack was walking along the school fence as all kids do.

Tracey

They were all playing Haunted Entry. Anyway, when he got to the Smith's garden, lazy Ann was in her garden waiting for him. She got hold of him and dragged him off the fence. Jack broke free and ran out of her garden and back home. He was in a terrible state when he got in. Next minute there is a knock on the door, it's the husband, Tosser Tom. He was trying to make out that it was all our Jack's fault. I told him it's a shame your wife didn't spend more time in the house, then she might see the dirt and filth clinging to the walls. I slammed the door in his face.

Joan
Good for you. The other week their youngest came to my front door with a rock and smashed my front window in. I haven't seen a penny.

Tracey
I don't think they ever forgave us when we all went round to theirs for a few drinks and your Raymond did his party piece by getting his hanky out and pretending there was dust everywhere. The handkerchief was black. We never got invited back again. Right, I better get on. I've got Charlene's boyfriend parents coming round.

Barbra
Are they the posh ones?

Tracey
That's them. They live in a big house near East Bridgford.

Barbra
Good luck with that and remember you are as good as anyone else. Money doesn't give you the right to look down on others.

Tracey
Thank you for that Barbra. Right I'll see you both later.

Tracey goes into her kitchen and starts to prepare some food for her visitors who are arriving for afternoon tea. As she is making the sandwiches and putting out the shop brought cake, she is smiling to herself thinking about Vain Vinnie. Jay walks into the kitchen.

Jay
Mum can I have a sandwich?

Tracey
No you can't. Now get yourself up them stairs and wash your hands and face. Then put your trousers and a shirt on.

Jay

Is royalty coming for tea?

Tracey

You could say that. Why did your sister have to pick this one for a boyfriend? Mark down the road is a good looking lad.

Jay

But his body odour leaves a lot to be desired.

Tracey

I could have bought him some deodorant. Tell your father to put a clean shirt on.

As Jay walks by the window to go upstairs, he spots his Grandma coming up the path.

Jay

(Shouting) Grandma is here.

Tracey

Bloody hell that's all I need. *(Tracey walks to the door and opens it)* Mother, it's nice to see you.

Doreen

That's a first.

Tracey

I've not seen you in that outfit before.

Doreen

This is my biker outfit. I've just ordered my Kawasaki too.

Tracey

Are you sure you're doing the right thing?

Doreen

Girl, when I'm on a motorbike doing speeds of a hundred miles per hour, it's like having the orgasm I've never had.

Tracey

Dad not with you?

Doreen

No, I've left him watching the snooker. If he thinks I'm going to sit there for hours while two men are hitting balls around a snooker table then he is very much mistaken. The only balls I would be hitting is your fathers, around the living room. With my foot.

Tracey

Your mouth gets worse.

Doreen

I'm not surprised, as it's so dry. *(She walks into the kitchen and sees all the sandwiches)* Having company are we?

Tracey

Yes, I've got Charlene's boyfriend's parents coming round.

Doreen

Are they the parents you said were stuck right up themselves?

Tracey

Mother please.

Doreen

(Picking up one of the sandwiches, she looks inside) I see you have brought salmon, it's a shame, it's not the red, but you have not expected to buy the best with that waster of a husband of yours.

Tracey

You know he is not well.

Doreen
He is well enough when he is drinking beer every night and smoking your fags. *(Doreen walks into the living room where she meets Jay)*

Jay
Hello Grandma.

Doreen
Hello my little darling, give your Grandma a kiss. *(Jay does this)* I'll just take a seat *(she sits at the side of the table which is placed at the back of the living room)*

George comes into the living room and sits on the sofa.

George
Hello Doreen.

Doreen
Hello George.

George
What sins have we committed to have you turn up on our doorstep?

Doreen
The sin of being a useless husband and father when it comes to my daughter and grandchildren.

George
Don't you think you are a bit old to be a biker.

Doreen
I'm sixty nine and more active than you have ever been.

George
Sixty-nine, that's a position that must be a distant memory for you?

Doreen
It's always been a distant memory for you George, seeing as your wife kicked you out of her bed years ago.

Jay
Mum they are here.

Tracey
(Coming out of the kitchen) Right you two, I want you both to be on your best behaviour.

There is a knock on the door, Tracey goes to open it.

Malcolm
Mrs Green, lovely to meet you.

Tracey
Please, call me Tracey.

Malcolm
I'm Malcolm and this is my wife Caroline.

Tracey
Do come in *(they all walk into the living room)* This is my husband George. *(They shake hands)* and my mother Doreen.

Doreen
Hello darling, how's it hanging?

Tracey
This is my son Jay.

Malcolm
Hello young man, are you the boy who will never be popular?

Tracey
I see Charlene has been talking.

Doreen

He is very popular with me, he is a super boy.

Tracey

Do sit down, George move up.

George

*(Sitting on the floor)*I like to sit on the floor by the door you get a cool breeze coming through.

Doreen

A lot of alcohol does warm you up.

Malcolm

Talking of alcohol I've brought you some beers. We usually bring wine but I thought you would appreciate the beer instead.

Tracey

That's very kind of you Malcolm.

Doreen

Throw me one over Mal, I'm as dry as Gandhi's flip flop.

Caroline

He likes to be called Malcolm.

Doreen

Amongst other names I'm sure Carol love. *(Doreen starts to laugh. Everyone else is straight faced)*

Malcolm

Unfortunately we can't stay as long as we had hoped. We have got the Bloomingdales coming to eat with us this evening. Caroline wants to make sure that everything is prepared for their arrival.

Doreen

Aren't they strippers?

Tracey
That's the Chippingdales.

Doreen
I went to see them once.

Caroline
Did you?

Doreen
I did, but I was disappointed.

Caroline
Why was that?

Doreen
They never took their undies off. I felt short changed. Lets be honest Carol love, we all want to see a good length swinging.

Tracey
I'll just get the sandwiches.

Malcolm
As you are dressed in leathers Mrs Crabs, would I be right in thinking you are a 'rocker'?

Doreen
I do love heavy rock Mel, but I'm more of a biker chick these days. I've just had a tattoo done on my arm.

Malcolm
Have you?

Doreen
I have. It's a skull with a snake coming out of the skulls mouth. I'm having a bat put on my leg next week, as my favourite song is 'Like A Bat Out Of Hell'.

Malcolm
Very nice Mrs Crabs.

Caroline
How does your husband feel about it?

Doreen
Who gives a toss Carol, it's my body.

Tracey
(Bringing in the food) Now in the sandwiches, I've got egg, potted meat and salmon and I've also got crisps and hoola hoops. Do help yourself.

Caroline picks up a sandwich and looks at her husband.

Malcolm
That's very kind of you, but we are having a five course meal to-night so we must leave some room.

Doreen
(Walking over to the food, she picks up one of the sandwiches and passes it to Malcolm) Have one of these pink salmon sandwiches and a packet of crisps. *(She throws him the crisps)*

Malcolm
Thank you Mrs Crabs.

Doreen
You're welcome love *(she belches)* better out than in Carol love. Throw me another of those beers, they are going down a treat. *(She passes Doreen a beer)*

Caroline
Have you been living here long Tracey?

Tracey

About twenty years.

Caroline

You used to live in one of these type of houses didn't you Malcolm?

Malcolm

I did, before I started the business. But when we were up and running I soon got out. I could never entertain my clients and friends in a place like this, they would think that my business has gone bust. *(He starts to laugh)*

Doreen

I'll let you know I raised three children in a house like this. They all turned out fine.

Caroline

That's good to hear.

Tracey

Anyone for a piece of cake?

Caroline

Did you make it yourself?

Tracey

I'm afraid not. I just don't have the time.

Caroline

If it was me I'd make sure I found the time. We must go, but before you do, can I just ask you is Charlene is on the pill? We wouldn't want our Robert being tricked into becoming a father. Especially as he has got such a glittering career ahead of him.

Doreen

When you are buying him a new car or designer clothes, buy him a packet of three. That way he won't be tricked as you call it.

Malcolm

Well we must leave you Mrs Green. Thank you for your hospitality.

Caroline

Goodbye Mrs Crabs.

Doreen

See you Carol love, thanks for the beer. *(She belches)*

Tracey shows them to the door and waves to them as they drive off. She then closes the door and walks back into the living room.

Tracey

Do you know Mother, for once could you have just keep your mouth shut. It's bad enough that I have to sit there and let these types of people look down on me because they think I'm so beneath them, but then to have my mother sit there drinking beer from a can belching every two minutes is disgusting. Also, their names are Caroline and Malcolm, not Mel and Carol. People of their class don't shorten their names.

Doreen

They didn't mind.

Tracey

Yes they did Mother, you only had to look at their faces.

Doreen

They are no better than us.

Tracey

Really Mother? That's why they can buy things and go places that I could only dream of. I go to work each day and sit behind a machine, making clothes that others can afford to buy, but not me and at the end of the week after everything is paid for I'm lucky if I've got a fiver left in my purse. A purse that's falling to bits.

George
You should be happy with what you've got.

Tracey
Should I George? Should I be happy that I have no money George despite how hard I work? Should I be happy George, that I have to buy second hand stuff and never be able to buy anything new? Should I be happy George when things go wrong in this house and we have to call your unqualified mate to fix things because he is cheap? For an hour you sat there and said nothing.

George
I didn't know what to say.

Tracey
You wouldn't, because you don't know anything. All you do is sit there and watch television for sixteen hours a day. Yes, you suffer from depression and anxiety, but that doesn't mean you can't pick yourself up a book and educate yourself and Jay, from now on I want you to put more effort into your school work because my lad, you will be going to university at eighteen.

Doreen
You don't belong with those sort of people.

Tracey
You might be right Mother, but I'll tell you that I do belong in doing something I would enjoy, that would allow me to use my brain. That's why I am going to take night classes so that I can go to university to become a social worker. While I'm doing this I'm going to volunteer to become a Samaritan. I might be poor and in my forties, but I'm going to work bloody hard to find the happiness I deserve. *(With tears in her eyes, Tracey storms out of the living room and into the garden)*

A Young Life Lost

Characters

Tina

A large woman in her mid twenties. She has limited education ability and has suffered abuse mentally and physically over her short life.

Beryl

A small hagged looking woman in her fifties. She is the mother of Tina, a daughter she abuses financially and mentally for her own gains.

Other characters

Tracey, Halima, Bet, Sally, Sandra, Miss Spears, Lesley B, Mr Thomas and Mr Husain.

Setting

The factory floor, Mr Thomas' office, outside the factory gate.

A Young Life Lost

It's lunchtime and Tracey, Sally and Bet are sitting around a table in the canteen.

Tracey
I have an announcement to make.

Bet
Don't tell me you are pregnant?

Tracey
Are you having a laugh?

Sally
What is it then?

Tracey
Well, you know I had Charlene's boyfriend's parents around the other week.

Bet
The posh gits who look down at other people from a great height?

Tracey
That's the ones. But despite their arrogance they got me thinking.

Bet
Thinking about what?

Tracey
Where my life is going and what I can do to change it.

Bet
Do you need to change it?

Tracey

I do Bet, I can't carry on making clothes that I can never afford to buy or sitting behind a machine, making them for the next twenty years thinking what if. It's time for me to use my brains again and open myself up to new challenges, challenges that make me feel I'm worth something to myself and to others.

Sally

So what have you done?

Tracey

I've enrolled on an Access Course which if I pass it will allow me to go onto university to become a social worker.

Bet

When is all this going to start?

Tracey

The course starts at the beginning of September.

Bet

So you are giving up work?

Tracey

I wish. As it is evening classes I will be able to do my work in the day. If the course needs me to work in the day I will use my holidays and my sick days.

Sally

There is going to be a lot of work you need to do and there won't be much time for socializing.

Tracey

When in the last twenty years did I have a social life? I know it is going to be hard going and I'm sure there will be times where I feel I want to drop out but I know this is my last chance and I'm determined to succeed.

Bet

If you pass and get to university how are you going to survive financially? Let's face it you couldn't carry on working here with all your uni work.

Tracey

I must admit that's a problem I haven't been able to solve at this time. But I've got a year to sort something out.

Bet

Knowing you something will turn up. Work hard and enjoy it my girl. Make us all proud.

At the other end of the canteen, Tina Tubs and her Mother are arguing.

Tracey

Here we go again.

Sally

What's the story behind those two?

Tracey

You have got Tina Tubs, who as you can see is a large woman. She is known as the local bike. In fact, before her weight ballooned, her nickname was Chopper named after the Chopper bike.

Sally

How did she put so much weight on?

Bet

As terrible as it is to say, if you brought her any type of food like cakes, biscuits, ice cream etcetera she was very happy to give you an hour of her time. It didn't take long for word to get around that you could buy a cake for a couple of quid and get rewarded for it. So the more men she had the more weight she put on. Hence the size you see today.

Sally

What about her Mother?

Bet

Now when it comes to the Mother, the word cougar comes to mind. When the young men went to see Tina in her bedroom, they would pass Tina the cake and the sex would begin. Now whilst this is going on Tina would be eating the cake at the same time, but if ever during the sex Tina finished the cake the sex was over and he was told to leave. It took the bloke ages to cotton on, that the bigger the cake the longer the sex. In the end they were bringing her wedding cakes to go the full distance. Anyway, with the no entry sign being put up, they blokes were frustrated as they weren't allowed to finish off. So when they left Tina's bedroom across the landing they saw a sign on her Mother's bedroom. 'This way for seconds.'

Sally

But she looks even worse than her daughter.

Bet

I agree, but the guys and especially the young guys were desperate to finish off. The Mother was responsible for an increase in the gay population on the estate.

Tracey

I better go and see what this argument is all about.

As Tracey walks over, both Tina and her Mother are seen fighting on the canteen floor. Tina is sitting on her Mother and slapping her in the face.

Tina

A slap for a slapper. Enjoy my seconds you filthy slut.

As Tina keeps slapping and pulling her Mother's hair, Tracey is trying to pull Tina off her Mother, but unable to get her off she calls for Bet and Sally. All three of them manage to drag Tina off. Lesley B runs over.

Lesley B
Beryl in my office now

Beryl
But-

Lesley B
Now. *(Tina goes to Lesley's office)*

Beryl
That bitch started it.

Lesley B
And this bitch has ended it. Who in their right mind ends up fighting their own daughter in their place of work?

Beryl
She just set upon me like a wild animal.

Lesley B
How did she get to be that wild animal Beryl? Was it because as a mother you used and abused your daughter throughout much of her life? Leaving her on her own as a child so you could get pissed in the pubs and clubs while your daughter had to sit on her own each night without food or electricity scared out of her wits.

Beryl
Well she is eating well now.

Lesley B
The more she ate the more you could open your disgusting legs to guys who were half your age. Not once did you ever show any love to-

wards your daughter. Get out of my sight you vile bitch before I forget where I am.

Beryl walks out of Lesley's office and Lesley slams the door.

Bet
Well you don't see that everyday.

Tracey
Come on girls, lets get back to work. *(As Tracey sits behind her machine, both Halima and Sandra come over to Tracey to give her a hug)*

Halima
Congratulations Tracey, you are going to make a great social worker.

Sandra
They won't know what's hit them.

Tracey
Thank you ladies, although there is a long way to go.

As she says this, applause can be heard all around the factory as everyone in the factory stands and faces Tracey. Tracey stands up and after waving at them all blows them a kiss.
Miss Spears comes out of her office.

Miss Spears
What is going on? Get back to work all of you. *(She marches up to Tracey)*

Bet
Watch out, the beast is approaching.

Miss Spears
Mrs Green, I believe you are responsible for this?

Tracey
Do you think so?

Miss Spears
I know so Mrs Green. I don't want to see this happening again until you complete your course. *(She puts a book on Tracey's table)* Now get on with your work. *(She walks away)*

Tracey lifts the book up and reads 'Social Work for Beginners.' Looking dumbfound, she looks at Bet.

Bet
Well you could knock me down with a feather. Today is definitely a day for firsts.

Halima
If I had not seen it with my own eyes, I would never have believed it.

Sandra
I knew there was a heart in there somewhere.

Lesley B walks over to Tracey.

Lesley B
Tracey love I want you to do me a big favour.

Tracey
Yeah of course?

Lesley B
At half past two, it's the disciplinary meeting for Tina. I want you to be at my side in the meeting.

Tracey
Are you sure? There isn't a lot I can say in her defence.

Lesley B

It's not for her benefit its for mine. If I haven't got you besides me to keep me in check I'm going to say or do something I regret. Now there is ten minutes before the meeting starts so go and have a fag and bring me a coffee.

Lesley B walks away towards the office and Tracey goes upstairs. Ten minutes later, Tracey walks down the factory floor holding a coffee.

Mr Thomas

Do come in Mrs Green and sit down *(Tracey does this, giving Lesley her coffee)* Miss Babbington has told us why she wants you in here, so I will tell everyone this is going to be a bumpy ride. Mrs Green, can you tell Miss Smith to come in. *(Tracey does this and two minutes later Tina enters the office and sits down)*

Tina

You're not going to sack me are you? Please don't, I've got nothing else. My mother will throw me out onto the streets if I can't pay my way.

Mr Thomas

Calm down Miss Smith. Now, precisely two hours ago you not only assaulted a member of staff, but you did it on my premises in front of a crowd of my employees, having their lunch break. What makes you think Miss Smith, that this behaviour would be tolerated?

Tina

She forced me to do it. She told me she wanted more money off me for my keep as her boyfriend, who she took off me, wanted to go on holiday.

Mr Thomas

That as it may be Miss Smith, but the fact is that you assaulted a worker in my factory, I cannot allow you to continue working here.

Lesley B

But before you pass sentence Mr Thomas, surely Miss Smith is allowed to tell us the life she has endured which led up to this assault?

Mr Husain

I don't think that would have any bearing on this meeting today.

Lesley B

(In a loud voice) Well I do Mr Husain, I believe it has a great bearing and I believe you should keep your opinion to yourself.

Mr Thomas

Miss Babbington that is enough.

Lesley B

No it is not enough, every condemned person has the right to speak before sentencing.

Mr Husain

You are talking like we are about to sentence Miss Smith to death.

Lesley B

That is just what you're doing.

Mr Husain

Don't be ridiculous.

Tracey

(Holding Lesley's arm) Mr Thomas, I agree what Miss Smith did was wrong, but behind every mistake there is a reason why that mistake happened, and as Miss Smith has worked her as a loyal and hard working employee for a very long time surely we should give her the chance to speak about the reasons behind her actions today.

Mr Thomas

I don't see the point, but as you wish.

Tracey

Tina what was your childhood like?

Tina

For what I remember, it was a very poor and lonely experience. Most of the time I would find myself in bed with several blankets around me to keep warm.

Tracey

Did you not have any gas or electric?

Tina

No, Mum would only have money for the pubs and clubs as she always came home steaming. The alcohol was her heating.

Tracey

What about food? Did you get much to eat?

Tina

Not really. At times our neighbour Mrs Parks would bring me round some food, but she was a single mother of four, so there was not much to go around. The times I went to school one of the dinner ladies took pity on me and gave me a bit extra, but with all the other children making fun of my shabby looks and my failure to read and write properly, I thought it was best to stay at home.

Mr Husain

Do we really need to hear this?

Lesley B

There's the door.

Tracey

So when you left school what did you do?

Tina

With my mum getting older, and her looks fading she made it known around the pubs that I was available for the right price. She also told them that I like to eat cake. I enjoyed eating the cake, especially as it was the first time I had regular food. I knew I was getting fat, but I didn't care. I had spent too many years feeling hungry. Four times I became pregnant but my mum phones social services each time. They took away my babies each time. I wanted to keep every one of them, but when you are still a teenager and have nothing, there wasn't much chance of keeping one, never mind four.

Tracey

What made you stop?

Tina

I got so many infections down below and with me becoming so fat the men stopped coming around. That's when mum got me a job here, so that I could keep earning money to fund-raise her nights out.

Tracey

So why the fighting in the canteen?

Tina

For the first time in my life I had a boyfriend. A boyfriend who wasn't just with me for that I had between my legs or for how much money I had in my purse. He was with me for me, as a person. But last week my mother took him out, on the money I gave her from my wages and got him drunk. She had sex with him behind one of the pubs she goes to. All my life Mr Thomas, I've only known people to take and use me. Don't take my job away Mr Thomas, please.

Miss Spears takes a tissue out of her bag and wipes away her tears.

Mr Thomas

I do sympathise with you Miss Smith, on what has happened in your life. But the fact is you hit another member of staff on these premises. I'm therefore terminating your employment as from now.

Lesley B

(Shouting) You cannot be serious. After all she has gone through you are just going to stab her in the back, like everyone else has in her life?

Mr Thomas

Mrs Green, take Mrs Babbington out and calm her down.

Tracey gets hold of Lesley and drags her out of the office. As she is dragged out, she continues to shout.

Lesley B

I hope you can live with yourself because I couldn't!

Tracey takes her to her office. Ten minutes later, Tina is seen going around the factory floor saying her goodbyes. She tells everyone she has got nothing now. Mr Husain comes across to Tina and tells her to get out as she is disturbing the workers. Tina goes to her locker and after putting everything into a plastic bag, she walks out of the factory gates . Five minutes later, one of the canteen staff races down the stairs to the shop floor and starts to scream. Everyone stops working and Lesley and Tracey run over to see why she is screaming.

Canteen lady

It's, Tina, she is hanging from a tree!

Lesley B

(Screaming) No!

Lesley and Tracey run up the stairs across the canteen and go outside. They both stop when they get to the tree Tina is hanging from. Lesley collapses onto her knees, where she is seen crying and screaming uncontrollably. After five minutes, Lesley picks herself up and runs inside the factory to Mr Thomas' office. She forcibly pushes the door open, smashing the glass as the door hits the wall.

Lesley B

(To Mr Thomas) Murderer, Murderer!

A Silver Lining

Characters

James and Lucy

Two young married people, who adopted one of Tina's children.

Martin

A young, good looking man in his late teens. He is the boyfriend of Charlene.

Other characters

Tracey, Sally, Bet, Halima, Sandra, Miss Spears, Mr Thomas, Lesley B, Jay and Charlene.

Setting

The canteen, Mr Thomas' office, Redhill Cemetery.

A Silver Lining

Sally walks up Tracey's path and knocks on the door.

Tracey

(Shouting from the top of her stairs) The door is open Sal, pour yourself a cuppa I'll be down in a minute.

Sally lets herself in and pours herself a cup of tea. Jay walks into the kitchen.

Jay

Hello Sally.

Sally

Good morning Jay, how's school?

Jay

School is fine, I've been getting top marks for a lot of my class work.

Sally

That is wonderful news.

Jay

The top of the class is where I want to be. Although, there is a girl in the year above me who keeps trying to come onto me. She asked 'do you play as hard as you work?' Then she started to rub her hands together.

Sally

What did you say?

Jay

I said I'm only focusing on my work at this time and you should get some cream for your dry hands, it will help with your dry skin.

Sally

I don't think her hands were dry.

Jay

In any case, she is not talking to me now.

Sally

At least you are consistent in your popularity.

Jay

My work is my best friend.

Sally

It will be for many years to come.

Tracey

(Walking into the kitchen) Morning Sally love.

Sally

Morning Tracey. You look very summery. That dress really shows off your figure.

Tracey

Thank you love. It was the roses and violets that attracted me to it.

Sally

Roses are red, violets are blue, it's time we shifted, so move it you. *(They both laugh)*

Tracey

(Walking out the door) Jay tell your father we need to spend some time sorting out the garden and tell your sister to get this house cleaned up before I come home.

Jay

I would do, but she is not here.

Tracey
Where is she?

Jay
She told me not to say.

Tracey
But-

Jay
Her boyfriend came round in his new car so she sneaked out at two minutes past ten last night.

Tracey
Miss Marple has got nothing on this one. As long as you stay popular to your school work, that's all that matters.

Tracey and Sally are seen walking down the hill when Mrs Jones comes running out of her garden.

Mrs Jones
Have you heard?

Tracey
Heard what?

Mrs Jones
They have taken that dirty git away.

Tracey
Which dirty git?

Mrs Jones
Terry Tucks at number ninety-five.

Tracey
What's he been up to?

Mrs Jones

Well, I'm not one for gossip.

Tracey

You never have been Mrs Jones.

Mrs Jones

But he was seen in the red light district.

Tracey

He wasn't?

Mrs Jones

He was. Rumour has it, it wasn't the first time.

Tracey

Well. He certainly painted the town red.

Mrs Jones

The Chinese see the colour red as a lucky colour. It wasn't that lucky for him and that dragon wife of his.

Tracey

She must be devastated.

Mrs Jones

It serves that snooty bitch right. She won't be able to look down her nose at anyone ever again. Do you know what she said to me the other day?

Tracey

What?

Mrs Jones

She announced that her eldest was getting married, and she said I don't know which wedding will be the best, ours or the royal wedding. She won't be complaining about my net curtains again.

Sally
We are going to be late.

Tracey
You're right, I'll see you later Mrs Jones, keep me informed.

Sally
(Walking down the hill) She seems bitter.

Tracey
She would be, her and Terry had an affair a while back which being a widower really ignited her sexual libido, so much so, she used to stalk him to the point they were having sex all over the place. Gardens, parks, behind walls and public toilets. They even had it on top of his car, the only trouble was though that it was parked at the side of the M1. Everyone was hooting their horn, one guy shouted 'there's not much wrong under that bonnet.' In the end, as frigid as his wife was, he couldn't leave her. Mind you, it was a good job she was frigid, as his manhood needed weeks to recover.

Both Tracey and Sally arrive at work and clock on. They both go and sit down behind their machines.

Bet
Don't get too comfortable Tracey love, the Beast from Bestwood wants to see you in her office.

Tracey
That's all I need.

Tracey walks down the factory floor and knocks on Miss Spears office.

Miss Spears
Come in Mrs Green.

Tracey

(Sitting down) Did you want to see me Miss Spears?

Miss Spears

I did. Firstly Mr Thomas would like you to represent Mrs Smith at this morning's disciplinary hearing. Of course, Miss Babbington would usually do it, but as you now she is on two weeks absence at this time.

Tracey

I don't think I can say much in her defence.

Miss Spears

Believe me Mrs Green, when it comes to defending that woman you not saying much will be more than most people could say.

Tracey

I thought she would be at home, getting ready for her daughter's funeral this afternoon.

Miss Spears

She was given the day off, but in her own words 'I would rather work this morning, as my selfish bitch of a daughter has left me needing to earn as much as I can.'

Tracey

The wrong woman died.

Miss Spears

Exactly. So if you could take your break at nine, that will give you a hour to prepare. Also Mr Thomas would like you to attend the funeral which starts at two.

Tracey

Does he?

Miss Spears

He does. It is believed that Miss Babbington will be there, so with the mother attending, he thought it would be best for you to keep and eye on Miss Babbington. You can go home to change as soon as Mrs Smith's disciplinary meeting is over. Will that be alright?

Tracey

That will be fine.

Miss Spears

Mr Thomas did say that if you agreed he would be very happy to give you an extra week's holiday next year. This will help you with your course.

Tracey

Do thank Mr Thomas for me.

Miss Spears

Just one more thing.

Tracey

Yes?

Miss Spears

Miss Mason.

Tracey

What about Miss Mason?

Miss Spears

She doesn't look well. Do you know what the problem is?

Tracey

I'm afraid not, but I'm planning to go round her's this weekend, so hopefully I can get some answers from her.

Miss Spears

I do hope so Mrs Green. We wouldn't want Miss Mason suffering in any way.

Tracey

We certainly wouldn't.

Miss Spears

I think it's your break time Mrs Green.

Tracey leaves Miss Spears office and goes up to the canteen with the rest of the gang. They get their food and sit down.

Bet

So what did the Beast of Bestwood want?

Tracey

Because Lesley is not here they want me to represent the Mother from Hell.

Bet

Good luck with that.

Tracey

I'll need more than good luck. How do you stick up for a woman who has been evil for so long?

Bet

Isn't it Tina's funeral this afternoon?

Tracey

It is, that's another thing because Lesley and the mother are going to be there, Mr Thomas wants me to attend, so I can keep an eye of Lesley.

Bet

Union rep in the morning, bodyguard in the afternoon. It's all good training.

Tracey

Are you around this weekend?

Bet

Any reason why?

Tracey

No reason, just thought It would be nice to pop round. Right ladies, should you not be getting back? It's only half a hour you have for your breakfast.

Halima

She thinks she's senior management now.

They all walk towards the door.

Sandra

Are you bothering?

Tracey

Not today, I've got a extra half a hour to prepare for my meeting.

Sandra

How are you going to prepare?

Tracey

With a couple of fags. *(They all laugh)* See you later.

Tracey goes off to have a fag. At around ten o'clock she is seen walking into Mr Thomas' office.

Mr Thomas

Good morning Mrs Green. It's so nice of you to help us out on this sad day. Now, before Mrs Smith comes in, you can see there is only myself and Mrs Spears in attendance. Mr Husain has agreed to manage one of my other interests, which leaves a vacancy. Now, I know you are looking to move into social work, but I would like you to consider the managerial job that is to be advertised.

Tracey

That is very kind of you Mr Thomas, but my heart is set on being a social worker. But there is someone who I think you should consider.

Mr Thomas

Who would that be?

Tracey

Mrs Docker. Now I agree, Mrs Docker's past history doesn't read well, but in her defence the domestic violence that Mrs Docker had to face on a daily basis would have had most women resorting to the extreme actions that she took. But let's not forget, Mrs Docker has worked in these types of establishments before. Even finding herself being a supervisor for a couple of years in one of them.

Mr Thomas

But would she be able to cope with the pressures of the job? Along with the new courses she would have to go on?

Tracey

In my honest opinion, yes.

Mr Thomas

Let's hope she will fill in the application form. Right lets have Mrs Smith in. *(Beryl Smith is called for and takes a seat)*

Beryl

Before we start, I just want to say that I'm innocent in all of this and didn't deserve being violently assaulted by Tina Smith.

Tracey

That is Tina Smith your daughter?

Beryl

When a daughter viciously assaults her mother, a mother who has put a roof over her head and supported her in all of her needs, then she is no daughter of mine.

Tracey

Would you say that your self-interests from the very start, took over your role as a mother?

Beryl

Just because I had a child doesn't mean my life should be put on hold.

Tracey

Not even for the well-being and safety of your child?

Beryl

What is it with all these questions?

Mr Thomas

Mrs Smith does have a point.

Tracey

I was just trying to establish why a daughter would want to attack her mother. A mother who says that she has always put her daughter first.

Beryl

I hope you are not saying that I was responsible for me getting beaten up?

Tracey

They always say, 'what goes around comes around.'

Mr Thomas

Although Mrs Smith's personal dealings with her daughter was, it seems, a major factor in Mrs Smith getting assaulted, we cannot hold

Mrs Smith accountable for what happened in the canteen.

Miss Spears

I agree with you Mr Thomas, but in the light of what has happened we can't expect Mrs Smith to go on working in a place where she would be reminded on a daily basis of the suffering she had to endure. If I'm right in thinking Mrs Smith, you got on very well with Mr Husain?

Beryl

I did Miss Spears.

Miss Spears

So well in fact that he thought you were one of the hardest workers here.

Beryl

I do work very hard.

Miss Spears

Well, as you probably don't know, Mr Husain has been appointed to manage one of Mr Thomas' interests on the other side of the estate, which if I'm right in thinking is much closer to where you live.

Beryl

It's just around the corner.

Miss Spears

Well with Mr Thomas' blessing I think you should be transferred. After all, Mr Husain needs hard working people like yourself. I have also heard he will soon be looking for a new supervisor. He needs you Mrs Smith, say will you go?

Beryl

As he needs me so much, I will go Miss Spears.

Mr Thomas

That is so kind of you Mrs Smith. I want you to pack up all your things and go home to prepare immediately for your new position. Thank you again Mrs Smith.

Beryl gets up and walks out of the office with a smile on her face.

Tracey

Thank you Miss Spears. I didn't know Mr Husain felt that way about Mrs Smith.

Miss Spears

He doesn't. The word loathing comes to mind. But as you said Mrs Green, what goes around comes around.

Mr Thomas

If you are going to be at the funeral by two Mrs Green, you best be off.

Half a hour later, Tracey walks up her garden path. As she opens her front door, she can hear noises coming from Charlene's bedroom.

Tracey

Charlene get down these stairs and bring your friend with you.

After five minutes, Charlene comes down the stairs with her boyfriend behind her.

Tracey

I can see by your face you are happy to see me. Martin, you've been going out with my daughter for a few months now, what are you intentions?

Charlene

Mum!

Martin

They are very honourable Mrs Green.

Tracey

That might have been before you got on top of her.

Charlene

Mum-

Tracey

You go to university in a couple of months, do you think your relationship will last?

Charlene

Of course it will. We love each other.

Martin

I hope so Mrs Green, but with the amount of work I've got to do, I won't have much of a social life. My parents are expecting great things of me.

Tracey

And Charlene?

Martin

We are having great fun together.

Tracey

Tell me you are using condoms?

Charlene

Mum stop it.

Martin

You can rest assured Mrs Green, I'm very careful.

Tracey

Make sure you are, as Charlene's fun will turn into a nightmare, as a one parent mother with no place to live. Right, I would love to carry on chatting but I've got a funeral to attend.

Tracey goes upstairs to change. Martin kisses Charlene and drives off. As Charlene comes back into the house, Tracey comes down the stairs dressed in black.

Charlene
You need to go to more funerals, that little black number suits you.

Tracey
If you don't start sorting your life out young lady, the next funeral will be yours.

Charlene
That's nice of you.

Tracey
Make sure you are at home tomorrow afternoon, it's time we sat down and discussed where your life is going.

Charlene
I'm going out Saturday afternoon.

Tracey
Not this Saturday afternoon. I'll see you later.

After lighting up a cigarette, Tracey leaves the house and walks down the hill towards Redhill Cemetery where the service is going to take place. After a fifteen minute walk, Tracey walks through the cemetery gates towards a small chapel in the cemetery grounds. Lesley is standing by the chapel door.

Tracey
You look as though you are miles away.

Lesley B
Hello Tracey love, I was just thinking on a beautiful day like today, why am I standing at a chapel door, waiting for a young woman to arrive in a coffin. A young woman who had her life ahead of her.

Tracey

Life at times is just so unfair.

Lesley B

For Tina, life was always unfair.

Tracey

At least her pain has stopped. Let's hope in her next journey she will find the happiness she deserves.

Lesley B

Fingers crossed, that her spirit will go into a new born baby, that will be given all the love it deserves.

Tracey

We are going deep.

Lesley B

That's what death makes you do. Anyway, how is everything at work?

Tracey

We had the mother from hell's disciplinary meeting this morning.

Lesley B

Don't tell me, she got a slap on the wrist and was told don't do it again?

Tracey

That was going to happen, but believe it or not, Spearsey convinced her that Mr Husain, who has been moved to another one of Mr Thomas' outlets on the other side of the estate needed her.

Lesley B

He hates her, she will be lucky if she lasts a week there.

Tracey

Thanks to Spearsey, she will get the justice she deserves. I must admit, there are times when that woman surprises me.

Lesley B

I'm afraid life has made her the hard bitter woman that you see today. At the age of five, she lost both of her parents in a car crash, a car that she was in at the time. She was taken in by an aunt, who hated Spearsey's mother because she stole, then married, the man she loved. So as you can imagine, her childhood was not the best. When she left school she signed up to go on a course to be a social worker, but she got herself pregnant. Her aunt told her if she had the baby then she must leave.

Tracey

That was evil.

Lesley B

The aunt saw it as revenge for what her sister had done to her. So without any money and no where to live, she had an abortion. She was never the same person after that. She gave up on her course, moved out of her aunt's place and got a job here.

Tracey

She gave me a book on social care. I wondered why.

Lesley B

I did hear you were thinking of changing careers.

Tracey

Lesley, if I don't do it now, it will be too late. I know it's going to be hard work, but if I don't try I'm just going to stay as I am, poor with no hope. Although the way Mr Thomas was talking they wanted me to apply for the manager's job.

Lesley B

You would be good as a manager, but much better as a social

worker. Don't allow anything to get in your way.

Tracey

What about you? Are you coming back?

Lesley B

I think after another week off, I'll be ready to come back. The bills don't pay themselves.

Tracey

Calling the boss a murderer to his face, I'm surprised you have a job to go back to.

Lesley

Me and the boss have been lovers for years.

Tracey

You don't say.

Lesley B

It never should have happened., but you can't control who you fall in love with. Yes, I know he is married with children, and yes, he has been promising to leave his wife for years.

Tracey

But his children should be grown up by now?

Lesley B

They are, but apparently his wife is not well.

Tracey

He just wants to have his cake and eat it.

Lesley B

You're right. For a long time I thought I was his icing on his cake, but as time went on, I discovered his wife had never stopped being the cherry on the top.

As they both stand at the chapel door, a young couple with a small child walks towards them.

Tracey
Good afternoon.

James
Good afternoon. We thought we were going to be late.

Tracey
Have you travelled far?

James
We live on the Isle of Wight.

Tracey
That's a beautiful place.

James
We like it.

Lesley B
Did you know the deceased?

James
No, we never met her. But we just felt like we had to come today to say thank you to a woman who has given us both such happiness, but allowing us a chance to have a child. We tried for many years without success, but then we had the chance to adopt our beautiful son.

Tracey
She would be very happy to know that her son was being brought up by two loving parents.

James
Thank you. *(They walk into the chapel)*

Tracey

You see, some good did come out of her sad life. There is another three children who have given Tina's life meaning.

The hearse pulls up and the pall bearers carry the coffin into the chapel with the mother from hell walking behind it. Tina's mother looks at Lesley with a grin on her face. Tracey holds Lesley's hand tightly.

Lesley B

Do we have to go in?

Tracey

We do. We will sit at the back and go before any of the mourners leave.

Walking arm in arm, they both walk into the chapel.

The Beginning Of The End

Characters

James Mason
A very good looking and intelligent lad, who had just turned sixteen. He is one of Bet's twin sons.

Other characters
Tracey, Bet, Barbra, Joan and Charlene.

Setting
Tracey's house and garden, Bet's garden.

The Beginning Of The End

Tracey is in the kitchen unloading the washing machine. Charlene is sitting at the kitchen table, eating her breakfast.

Tracey

Why is it, every weekend I'm on my knees unloading the washing machine like Cinder-bloody-rella. What hope have I got, that a prince will knock at my door.

Charlene

You have got Dad.

Tracey

As I said, what hope have I got that a prince will knock at my door.

Charlene

Right, I'm off.

Tracey

You're going no-where lady.

Charlene

But Mum-

Tracey

Don't Mum me my girl. I told you that Saturday we were going to talk and that's just what we are going to do.

Charlene

I'm meeting Sophie in half an hour.

Tracey

You better phone her and tell her you are having communications with your mother.

Charlene

This is so humiliating.

Tracey

I'm just going to hang out the washing and I'll be back, so don't even think about going anywhere.

Tracey goes into the garden and starts to peg out her washing.

Barbra

(Coming into her garden) Hello Tracey love.

Tracey

Hello Barbra, what brings you out?

Barbra

With the weather being so nice, I thought I would do a bit of gardening.

Tracey

I asked my George earlier in the week to do some gardening but it's like talking to a brick wall.

Barbra

Well, I have seen him in the garden. In fact, he has never been out of it all week.

Tracey

He is trying to become a literary genius.

Barbra

What's that when it is at home?

Tracey

He can't stop reading books. Last week I said has anyone seen my handbag and he replied 'a handbag,' he had been reading "The Importance of Being Earnest.' He keeps calling me Miss Bennent, her from

Pride and Prejudice. Yesterday I said do you want a drink and he said 'I do - shaken not stirred.'

Barbra

Did you tell him his Oscar is in the post?

Tracey

It won't be in the post, but somewhere else where the sun don't shine. *(They both laugh)* How did your bunions go?

Barbra

They went very painfully. I was walking on my hands and knees for two days. I caught him looking at my bottom every time I crawled past him. I said to him, what are you looking at? Do you know what he said?

Tracey

What?

Barbra

He said as your feet are out of action, it will be good to explore new territory. I told him, you go anywhere near my bottom and my fist would be exploring your mouth.

Tracey

With your feet out of action, along with his mouth, it will be like having a foot and mouth disease for him.

Barbra

And you know what they do to cows with foot and mouth?

Tracey

His days are numbered.

Barbra
Days? Don't you mean minutes. (They both laugh)

Joan

(Coming out of her garden with a pile of washing) Hello ladies.

Tracey

Hello Joan. You are not washing again?

Joan

What can I do when I have a teenage boy. Look at those sheets, they are as stiff as a board.

Barbra

Too much information.

Joan

Well as least what he is doing is keeping the sheets white, not like that diarrhoea episode. They wouldn't use my sheets to advertise how good their cleaning products are for getting rid of stains. If they did they would go bankrupt in a week.

Tracey

Did I tell you about Miss Lowe?

Barbra/Joan

No.

Tracey

Well you know she has been having trouble with her water works.

Barbra

Yes, we all thought it was thrush do to the fact she was tinder dry.

Joan

I told her the other day, what ever you do make sure you don't drop a match down there when you are lighting up a fag.

Tracey

Anyway. She had one of those phone consultations with her doctor, although it wasn't her own doctor, he's up in court for sexual misconduct.

Joan

I heard something about that.

Tracey

Young woman were going to see him with minor problems and he was telling them to remove their clothes as they needed a full examination.

Barbra

The filthy git.

Tracey

So this student doctor comes on the phone and started asking her questions. He said how much alcohol do you consume in a week. Then he asked her how many partners have you had and do you practise safe sex.

Barbra

He didn't?

Tracey

She told him if my pension could stretch to it, I would be pissed every day. At ninety-two, I would tell them to forget the condoms as every minute counts at my age. *(They all burst out laughing)* Right I'll see you both later.

Tracey walks into the kitchen and sits down at the kitchen table with Charlene.

Charlene

I'm meeting Melanie in a hour.

Tracey

You hope. Right my girl, its time we sort out where you are going in your life, because at the moment you are going no-where, other than your bed which you spend half your day in.

Charlene

You know after my A-levels I was going to have a year off from studying.

Tracey

That's right. But we agreed that you would work for the first six months then go travelling the second six months. We didn't agree that you would spend six months in your own bed and the next six months in your boyfriend's bed.

Charlene

Mum-

Tracey

Don't mum me. You either go to university or you get a job, it is your choice. But if you think you are going to swan around like you have been doing, then you can think again. Another thing while we are doing the mother, daughter chat, what is going on with you and your boyfriend?

Charlene

What do you mean what's going on?

Tracey

He goes to university in a couple of months. Do you honestly think a good looking nineteen year old who is going away for three years will want to be going out with a girl who still lives on a council estate and has no money?

Charlene

Are you saying I'm not good enough?

Tracey

In my eyes you are as good as anyone else, but for people who live in the rich parts, they tend to look down on people like us.

Charlene

My Martin is not like that.

Tracey

You might not think he is, but when he has the sort of parents he has got then he is expected to marry a girl from a family that has money and a position in society.

Charlene

Where is love in all of this?

Tracey

As Tina Turner says, what's love got to do with it. It is all about the status a marriage will bring.

Charlene

So if a guy is wealthy, has status , but is grotesque the girl will say yes when he asks her to marry him?

Tracey

She will and if it's the other way around he will. Why do you think that the mistress plays a big part in the lives of the wealthy. As long as it stays behind closed doors then those around them will turn a blind eye.

Charlene

So what you are saying is that a girl like me has to stay in my own class.

Tracey

There is nothing wrong with being working class, in fact I've always been proud of being working class, but there is one way you can jump up a class.

Charlene

What's that?

Tracey

Through education and going to university.

Charlene

So I've got to go to university to keep my boyfriend?

Tracey

Normally, I would say a person goes to university because it allowed the person to go through many more doors when it comes to choosing a profession that will pay at least three times more than a working class wage. This will enable them to buy bigger and better every time, but in your case, yes. If you love him enough.

Charlene

I do.

Tracey

That's sorted then.

Charlene

So I'm going to university to keep my boyfriend.

Tracey

Only if you think he is worth it.

Charlene

He is.

Tracey

That's great news. I've sorted three universities out for you and set up your interviews for next week.

Charlene
Mum.

Tracey
Now here is fifty pounds which will cover your travel expenses. If you go to the one I think you will go to, then I've got you a place in their halls of residence for the first year.

Charlene
Are you sure you don't want to do the course for me?

Tracey
I would do but your boyfriend, although beautiful, is a bit too young for me.

Charlene
(Laughing) Just a bit.

Tracey
I'll slap your legs young lady. *(They both laugh)* Now come and give your mother a hug. *(This they do)*

The next day Tracey is seen walking up Bet's path. She knocks on the door and James opens it.

Tracey
Hello you beautiful boy.

James
Hello Aunty Tracey. Mum is in the garden.

Tracey
Wonderful. How is she?

James
I'm a bit worried about her. She is losing a lot of weight which is making her look very gaunt looking in the face.

Tracey

Right, lead me to her and do me a favour, open up the bottle and bring us a couple of glasses out. *(She passes the bottle of wine to James)*

They both walk out into the garden.

James

Mum, Aunty Tracey is here. *(There is no reaction from Bet)*

Tracey

Go and pour the wine and leave your mother to me.

James goes back into the kitchen and Tracey goes to sit next to Bet.

Bet

Hello Tracey love, I was miles away.

Tracey

Don't tell me, you were on a beautiful Caribbean island running down the beach holding the hand of a beautiful young woman.

Bet

Try walking down the beach, my running days went years ago. So what brings you round?

Tracey

You.

James brings out two glasses of wine.

Bet

What's going on here?

Tracey

It's a beautiful day, the birds are flying around and your flowers look beautiful. So what would be nicer than a couple of mates sitting in the garden drinking a glass of wine?

James goes back into the kitchen.

Bet
Cheers.

Tracey
Cheers. Now how are you keeping?

Bet
I'm good. In fact my weight loss, due to me dieting, has given me so much more energy. There are days I could run a marathon.

Tracey
Is that a fact?

Bet
It is.

Tracey
You don't think I've come round here to sit in you garden for a couple of hours listening to you talking crap do you?

Bet
What do you mean?

Tracey
I mean, anyone with a single brain cell can see you're not well.

Bet
I don't know what you're talking about-

Tracey
You don't? Well then tell me why did Louie come round to my house the other day to tell me about you having to run to the toilet

every five minutes and why he could hear you being as sick as a dog. I believe there are other times when you don't reach the toilet and wet yourself. Do you know what I'm talking about now? Before I took a step through your door, James is telling me that he is worried about how much weight you have lost and how gaunt you are looking. So don't sit there and tell me you don't know what I am taking about. I have booked you to see the doctor at nine tomorrow morning. I'll be here at half past eight on the dot. So make sure you are ready and don't even think about not opening the door because if you don't I'll smash it in and drag you out by your frigging hair. *(In a quiet voice)* Right my darling, I've got to go. I'll see you tomorrow. *(Tracey kisses Bet on the cheek and walking into the kitchen where she hugs James)*

James

Bye Aunty Tracey.

Tracey

Bye my darling. Keep your chin up.

Tracey walks out of the door and James walks into the garden.

James

Bloody hell I wouldn't want to get on the wrong side of her.

Bet sits looking into space. As she does, a tear falls down her cheek.

The Ending Of One
The Beginning Of Another

Characters

Louie Mason
Like his twin brother, he is a very good looking and intelligent lad. But unlike his twin, he is gay.

Mrs Johnson
A medium size woman in her fifties. She is the wife of Terry who has been having an affair with Mrs Jones.

Doctor June
A small woman in her early sixties. She has been the local doctor for years, therefore she knows everyone in the community.

Jinny Jucie
A small woman in her mid sixties. She is very open minded and enjoys the company of men.

Rachel
A woman in her mid fifties. She is the receptionist at the doctors surgery. She has a problem controlling her laughter.

Other characters
Tracey, Bet, Mrs Jones, Halima, Sandra, Sally, Brenda, Lesley B and Miss Spears.

Setting
Doctors surgery, canteen, factory floor.

The Ending Of One
The Beginning Of Another

At exactly eight thirty Tracey knocks on Bet's door. Bet's son Louie opens the door.

Louie

Morning Aunty Tracey.

Tracey

Morning flower. Is your mum ready?

Louie

She is on her way. She had a bad night last night,

Tracey

Did she?

Louie

She was running to the toilet every five minutes.

Tracey

Fingers crossed she will be back walking to the toilet soon.

Bet

(Coming to the door) Good morning Tracey.

Tracey

Good morning Bet. Come on girl we are going to be late.

Both Tracey and Bet walk down the hill, Mrs Jones comes out of her front garden.

Mrs Jones

Have you heard?

Tracey

Heard what?

Mrs Jones

He got two years.

Tracey

He didn't?

Mrs Jones

That's what you get when you are married to a frigid bitch. I hear she is putting the house on the market. Either that or die of shame.

All of a sudden Mrs Johnson, the wife of Terry, the convicted curb crawler, comes rushing out of her garden.

Mrs Johnson

The reason he got no sex from me was because after touching a dirty slapper like you, I could never let him touch me again. He preferred to have prostitutes rather than touch you again. Well at least they were cleaner and better looking than an old scrubber like you. When we started dating he took me to the best hotels, where did he take you? Public toilets? No-one would ever spend a penny on you.

Mrs Jones

Well at least I didn't put super glue on my legs.

Mrs Johnson

Well with the smell of fish coming from your freebie minge, he should have covered your fat thighs with a gallon of super glue. No wonder he never had fish from the chip shop ever again after being with you.

Both women continue to argue while Tracey and Bet slip away and continue to walk down the hill.

Tracey
Well you don't see that everyday. It's not even nine o'clock yet.

Both ladies go into the doctors surgery and sit down. Jinny Juice is sitting opposite them.

Jinny
Hello Tracey love.

Tracey
Hello Jinny. I've not seen you for ages, how have you been?

Jinny
I'm fine pet. You know I lost my Burt?

Tracey
I did hear. I heard you were on holiday at the time?

Jinny
We were. We went to Spain with the Swingers Association. We like to go to the other countries to experience different cultures.

Tracey
What country did you find the best?

Jinny
That's a hard one. *(The receptionist, Rachel, begins to laugh while everyone else is stony faced)* Probably the Italians. They are very passionate lovers. Make sure you avoid the Germans, it's wam bang thank you man, and as for the Americans they like to talk the whole way through which can give you a headache.

Tracey
So how did he die?

Jinny

Well, the Swingers Association likes to put on excursions for the groups, so we went to a strip club that lays on the entertainment. One of the acts was Ping Pong Penny who shoots so many. Although this night she used golf balls. As she started firing, Burt forgot to duck and one of the gold balls hit him on the forehead. He collapsed and never regained consciousness again. *(The receptionist Rachel can be heard laughing. Everyone turns to look at her)*

Tracey

That's horrible. Did it cost much to bring him home?

Jinny

It would have cost a fortune if I had.

Tracey

So is he still here?

Jinny

We didn't take out any medical insurance and what with the price of funerals today, I thought the best thing would be to leave him there. He would have wanted it that way. It was months before I could get back to my swinging ways. But do you know Tracey, I'm so glad I went back because while I was away we had some new members, one of them was my Harold. The first time we did it, we just clicked so I'm here to see if we can start a family. *(Again, the receptionist Rachel starts to laugh. Everyone turns to stare at her)* He is ten years older than me, so we thought it would be best to start straight away.

Tracey

Do you think you might have left it a bit late?

Jinny

I know, I'm sixty-five, but I'm still mentally and physically fit. He is here now.

Harold walks into the Doctor's surgery using a zimmer-frame. The receptionist Rachel explodes with laughter, tears streaming down her face

Tracey

(Whispering to Bet) He could give the elephant man a run for his money.

On the loudspeaker, Bet is told to go to room number one. Both Tracey and Bet walk past the receptionist Rachel, who is laughing uncontrollably on the floor and goes to room one.

Doctor June

Good morning Bet, and I see you have brought Tracey with you *(they sit down)* now what can I do for you?

Bet just sits there and says nothing.

Tracey

Bet, as you can see, has not only lost a lot of weight due to the fact that she eats very little and what she does eat comes back up again, but is also having trouble when she goes to the toilet.

Doctor June

Is this right Bet? *(Bet says nothing)* I can't help you if you are not going to say anything.

Bet

There is nothing to say, I feel fine.

Doctor June

Well, lets do your blood pressure and we will take a little blood. After which I will give you a smear test.

Bet

There's no need Doctor.

Doctor June
Just to be on the safe side. Pop yourself onto the bed. *(She draws the curtains)*

Five minutes later, Doctor June opens the curtains and Bet returns to her seat.

Tracey
You alright love? *(Bet says nothing)*

Doctor June
I will send these off to the lab and I should get the results back in a couple of days. I will ring you when they arrive, Thank you ladies.

Tracey and Bet walk out of Doctor June's room and past the reception, where Rachel is being attended to by one of the doctors. Receptionist Rachel is having breathing problems due to the excessive laughter.

Tracey
(Outside) I think it might be best if you don't go into work this afternoon. I'll tell Spearsey. You go home and sit in your garden this afternoon. You could do with a bit of sun on you.

Bet
Thank you Tracey.

They both hug and Bet is seen walking up the hill. Tracey walks to work. When she gets there, she goes upstairs to the canteen. Miss Spears comes from the toilet and sits down with Tracey.

Miss Spears
How did it go Mrs Green?

Tracey
Not very well. Bet hardly said a word and the expression on the

doctor's face, she couldn't hide her concern.

Miss Spears
When will they get the results back?

Tracey
The doctor said in a couple of days, I think she will have to go and have more done at the City Hospital.

Miss Spears
Not looking good then?

Tracey
Let's just say, I don't think there will be a happy ending.

Miss Spears
Let her know, she can have as much time off work as she needs. When her appointment comes through, let me know and I will book you both off, on full pay of course.

Tracey
That's very kind of you.

Miss Spears
You stay up here and have your lunch, if I say so myself Brenda makes a mean quiche Lorraine. I'll see you later.

Miss Spears walks off to the shop floor while Tracey goes up to the counter to get her lunch.

Brenda
Hello love, you having an early lunch?

Tracey
I've just come back from the doctors. I couldn't leave Bet on her own.

Brenda
How did it go?

Tracey
Not too well. She gets the results back in a couple of days.

Brenda
Let's keep our fingers crossed. I'll make up a food hamper for her. It will help her to keep her strength up.

Tracey
That's kind. I hear your quiche Lorraine is to die for?

Brenda
It is only second to my youth and beauty.

Tracey
Everything comes second to that.

Brenda
You smooth talker you. *(She puts a piece of quiche Lorraine on a plate with some salad and gives it to Tracey)* That's on me love.

Tracey
You are a star.

Tracey sits down at a table. Five minutes later Sally, Halima, and Sandra walk through the canteen doors.

Halima
I see the part-timer has returned.

Tracey
Hello girls.

Sandra
What is the quiche like?

Tracey
Bloody lovely.

Sally
It's a shame Bet's not here. She would love that.

Sandra
I don't know about the quiche, but she would love the Lorraine.

Halima
(Raising her voice) Brenda can we have three quiches?

Brenda
Okay love, I'll bring them over.

They all sit down.

Sally
How is Bet?

Tracey
Not very good. The doctor took her blood pressure and some of her blood. The results should come back in a few days. I think the smear was the most uncomfortable thing she had to endure. I must admit though, I've got a bad feeling about this. You only had to look at the doctors face to know that something was wrong.

Halima
All we can do is to be there for her.

Tracey
Now before I forget, as you know with the departure of Mr Husain.

Halima
The way he treated poor Tina, good riddance.

Tracey

There is now a job vacancy for the general manager's job.

Sandra

What's that got to do with us?

Tracey

Well, talking to Mr Thomas before the mother from hell meeting, I recommended Sally for the job.

Sally

Don't be silly, with my past record there is not a chance in hell.

Tracey

Don't be so sure love. He knows about your spell inside, but he also knows about your past experience in the trade. So although he didn't say the job was yours he would be very happy if you applied for it.

Sally

Don't be daft.

Halima

You are as good as anyone.

Sandra

Believe me, if Mr Thomas didn't want you to apply, he would tell you.

Tracey

Now here is the application form, fill it in and give it to Spearsey by Friday.

Sally

Really?

Tracey/Halima/Sandra

Really.

Tracey

Right come on you lot, you get paid for working not talking.

Halima

Hark at the part timer.

With smiles on their faces they walk down the stairs and sit behind their machines. Lesley B comes up to Tracey.

Lesley B

Hello love, nice of you to join us. I hear it's not looking too good for our Bet?

Tracey

If you ask me I don't think she will be here this time next year.

Lesley B

Still so young. She has phoned in sick for the rest of the week. But Mr Thomas did say she can have as much time off as she needs. Did you give Sally the application form?

Tracey

I did.

Lesley B

Sally love.

Sally

Yes.

Lesley B

Make sure you get that application form in to Miss Spear's first thing Friday.

Sally

But-

Lesley B
Don't but me love, just do it.

Lesley B walks away and as she walks past Mandy. Mandy shouts out.

Mandy
Lesley, there is a pool of water under my machine and my leggings are all wet *(she starts to moan)* what is happening please help me.

Lesley B
(Shouting) Tracey get down here now.

In a flash Tracey runs down to Mandy's machine.

Tracey
Okay Mandy, everything is going to be fine.

Lesley B
Don't tell me she is going to give birth.

Tracey
She is and way soon by the looks of it.

Miss Spears
(Coming out of her office) What the hell is going on?

Lesley B
(Shouting) Phone an ambulance now.

Miss Spears
Right. *(Rushing back into her office)*

Tracey
Run up the stairs and get Brenda down here, she has delivered a few in her time.

Lesley dashes up the stairs and pushes the door back.

Lesley B
(Shouting loudly) Brenda get your ass downstairs now.

Brenda
What the bloody hell is going on?

Lesley B
(Shouting even louder) Now Brenda!

Brenda
(Rushing out of the kitchen they both rush downstairs to where Mandy is) It's alright my love. I know it hurts, but as soon as we get this baby out the sooner the pain will go. Lesley go to my kitchen, I want some hot water, towels, and the pegs that are holding up the tea towels on the line. Move girl. *(Lesley rushes off)* Tracey get that table over there and bring it here.

Tracey
I'm on it. *(Shouting)* Girls give me a hand.

Halima, Sandra and Sally rush over to the table and all four of them carry it over to where Mandy is. As they bring the table over, Lesley B brings a bucket of hot water, towels and some pegs.

Brenda
Right ladies, help me lift her onto the table and don't forget to bend your knees as you are lifting. With this weight you don't want to put your back out.

Each one of them gets hold of a leg or an arm and lifts Mandy onto the table.

Tracey
Bloody hell, you will have to stop her ordering double chips and pie Brenda.

Brenda

You are taking the piss, she is my best customer. Right ladies, grab a peg and put it on your nose, its time for those leggings to come off.

As Brenda takes Mandy's leggings off, there is a gasp from the rest of the workers in the factory. They are seen retreating backwards spraying themselves with perfume from their handbags as they go. Brenda goes and has a look between Mandy's legs.

Tracey

How's it looking?

Brenda

Lesley bring me the bucket.

Lesley B

I thought that hot water is normally needed after the birth?

Brenda

Normally yes, but looking at the state of it down there, it needs it now. Not even lipstick could hide the mess those lips are in. Right Mandy, it is time to push.

With everyone encouraging her, Mandy starts to push. After five minutes, the babies head appears.

Tracey

The head is out, one last push Mandy.

Mandy gives one last push and the baby comes out.

Brenda

Well done my darling. *(Brenda picks up the baby and puts her in Mandy's arms)* You have a beautiful baby girl. Any ideas on what you are going to call her?

Mandy

I haven't thought about it at all.

Brenda

(Taking the peg off her nose) Why not call her Peggy?

Mandy

I like that name.

Brenda

Peggy it is then. *(Facing the workers)* Everyone, it's a girl called Peggy.

Everyone starts to clap and cheer as the ambulance men walk towards Mandy.

Who's The Daddy?

Characters

Dirty Mouth Deb

A small woman in her sixties. When she talks, every other word is a swear word. She tells it as she sees it, and she does this very loudly.

Other characters

Tracey, Sally, Brenda, Sandra, Halima, Lesley B, Maxi-Bates, Mr Thomas and Miss Spears.

Setting

The factory canteen, Lesley B's office, Mandy's house.

Who's The Daddy?

At lunch time, the next day everyone gather in the canteen for a meeting.

Lesley B

(Banging the table) Thank you everyone for attending. *(Some people are still talking)*

Deb

Shut the fuck up. *(Everyone cheers)*

Lesley B

Now as you know, yesterday a beautiful baby girl was born in our factory which makes that child not only one of us but our responsibility that she is looked after and cared for by her aunts and uncles that are here today. Now as you know, Mandy is not the cleanest of women.

Sandra

That's an understatement.

Deb

She would give the rats a run for their money. *(Everyone laughs)*

Lesley B

However, she has given birth to our niece, so it makes us responsible for her health and well-being. Now if anyone has ever been brave enough to go into Mandy's place *(everyone gasps)* then you will know that it's a place where the bubonic plague could have started. So with such a filthy place, we cannot allow our new baby to be brought up there. So after work today, everyone will assemble outside Mandy's gate with buckets and mops. This will allow us to get rid of the rats forever. *(Everyone cheers)* Now we have made up a list of all the things that need doing, so if you can tick on the sheet which ones you can help with that will be greatly appreciated. Now Mr Thomas, who will be outside Mandy's gate tonight, has said that tomorrow morning will be given over to the making of different outfits for baby Peggy. The store cupboards will be open for you to use any fabric's you need. *(Everyone claps at Mr Thomas' generosity)* One last thing, if it hadn't been for one particular person who showed how amazing she was throughout the birth, then I'm sure we wouldn't be standing in this canteen today. The wonderful Brenda everyone. *(Everyone claps and cheers. Lesley B waves Brenda over.)* Now we have had a whip around and brought you some flowers and a drop of the hard stuff.

Brenda

Thank you everyone. If any of you ladies feel you need to push, just give me a shout. *(Everyone claps)*

Lesley B

Thank you everyone. I'll see you all outside Mandy's gate at five. Don't forget your pegs, as you won't make it inside the house without them.

Everyone disappears as they head back out to their jobs. As Tracey sits down behind her machine, Lesley B comes up to her.

Tracey

Are you alright love?

Lesley B

I'm fine pet, have you got a minute?

Tracey

Yes of course.

Lesley B

(Both walking over to Lesley's office, they take a seat) A couple of things. It's alright for us to give Mandy's place a spring clean, but we need someone who can give Mandy a spring clean as well. We need

someone who can advise her in the ways of cleanliness and healthy eating. She does need to loose some weight.

Tracey

Did you say some?

Lesley B

(Laughing) I was being kind. I was going to ask you, but come September you are going to be up to your eyes in it. Anyone you can think of?

Tracey

Do you know, there is someone.

Lesley B

Who?

Tracey

Miss Spears.

Lesley B

Really?

Tracey

Well, she lives on her own, and I don't think she has much of a social life. So she has the time and she was going to be a social worker. Ask her and see what she says.

Lesley B

Go on then.

Tracey

She can only say no. What was the other thing on your mind?

Lesley B

Who is the father?

Tracey

I must admit that got my thinking as well.

Lesley B

I think it's one of the blokes that work here. Now normally with some of the women who work here, it would be impossible to find out, due to the fact that they put the s into slut, but in Mandy's case, no bloke can get near her and if they did they couldn't hold their breath long enough before they ejaculated.

Tracey

Do you know Lesley love you are right. So it would have to be some-one who was not only pissed, but is gagging for sex twenty-four seven.

Lesley B

It can't be.

Tracey

Surely not?

Lesley B

(On the tannoy) Can Max Bates come to the union office.

Two minutes later, Max is standing outside Lesley's door. Lesley waves him in.

Lesley B

Come in Max and have a seat.

Maxi-Bates

(Sitting down) You wanted to see me?

Lesley B

We did. I won't beat about the bush Max, Tracey and I was talking about Mandy and the baby and was wondering who the father was.

Maxi-Bates

What does that have to do with me?

Lesley B

Everything. Seeing as we believe it is you.

Maxi-Bates

It could be a hundred and one blokes, so why are you blaming me?

Lesley B

You're right, it could be a hundred and one different blokes, but this is Mandy we're talking about. So it would have to be someone young who couldn't take their drink and someone who thinks about sex twenty-four seven.

Tracey

Max we are not here to criticise or to judge you. Let's be honest, we all make mistakes. We both know if you are found out about having sex with Mandy then you will be ridiculed for years. But there is a beautiful baby girl involved now, who one day will have the right to know who her father is.

Lesley B

How did you get in that situation?

Maxi-Bates

It was my mate's birthday and we were hitting the shots, by twelve o'clock I was hammered. So when I left the pub, I headed for the chippy where I ordered chips with curry. While I was waiting, I saw Mandy walking out with pie and double chips. When I got outside, Mandy had finished eating, but was still hungry. So she came onto me for my chips. Feeling a lot of movement down below, I went to put my hand in my pocket, but remembered the trousers I had on were pocket-less, Mandy snatched my chips and curry and grabbing my shirt collar pulled me around the back of the chippy. Bending over she said 'You can take me from behind as I'm eating my chips and curry. With downstairs dictating, I was powerless, and had to obey what my penis was telling me. A few minutes later, Mandy had finished eating the chips and curry and was asking me to buy her some more chips. When I said I hadn't got any more money, she pushed me away and said "if you can't feed me you can't breed me." But those few minutes gave me enough time to put out the fire below. If only I had trousers with pockets in. What am I going to do Tracey? If I had to marry Mandy my life would be over and what I earn here, there's no way I can afford to bring up a child.

Tracey

Normally, I would say you should of thought about that, but seeing as both my children were made because of demon drink, I know where you are coming from. Also for a lad of nineteen. It's not fair that one mistake should ruin his life. So what I suggest is that you set up a trust fund for Peggy and each week or month, put in it what you can afford, so when Peggy turns eighteen, you can give her the trust fund in order to help her with what she wants to do with her life.

Lesley B

That's a brilliant idea. Don't worry Max, what is said in this room stays in this room.

Maxi-Bates

Thank you so much.

Lesley B

Right you two, any chance of you doing any work this afternoon?

Tracey

(Laughing) We would love to but its clocking off time.

Maxi-Bates

I'll see you both at five. *(IIe walks out of the office)*

Tracey
Don't forget to talk to Spearsey.

Lesley B
I won't, leave it to me.

Tracey walks out of the office and clocks off. Two hours later, Tracey walks down the hill to Mandy's place. She can see a large crowd has gathered outside Mandy's gate. Everyone cheers as she walks towards them.

Tracey
(With a big smile on her face) I didn't think this many people would turn up,

Next minute Brenda parks up in a van, opening the door, it reveals it is full of everything that is needed to clean Mandy's house.

Brenda
Right, help yourself everyone. *(They all do.)*

Tracey
Right, if I was you get into groups around five and pick a room.

Just before they go in, Mr Thomas parks up in his Mercedes. As he gets out of his car he is seen wearing a pair of dungarees and rubber gloves on his hands. Laughing, everyone starts singing Come on Eileen. After they have finished singing, Lesley B goes to the door and opens it.

Lesley B
Right everyone, pegs on and charge.

Everyone rushes in and soon gets down to cleaning every room. In the kitchen, Tracey shouts Brenda over.

Brenda

What's up love?

Tracey

Looking at this fridge-freezer and the cooker, she is going to have to have new ones. Now as you know we had a whip around this morning and made around five hundred pounds, do you think your Gary can help?

Brenda

For that type of money love, he would give up his own blood to help Dracula.

Tracey

By the looks of it in the garden, it needs some attention.

Mr Thomas

(Who is standing next to Tracey) When they finish the garden, send me the bill.

Tracey

That's very kind of you Mr Thomas.

Mr Thomas

Baby Peggy belongs to us all now. How is Miss Mason doing?

Tracey

Not very well. I had a phone call from one of her boys this morning. The hospital wants her to go in tomorrow afternoon. They want to x-ray her and do a couple of tests. But if you ask me Mr Thomas, I'll be surprised if she's still here with us by Christmas.

Mr Thomas

That is sad. She has two young boys doesn't she?

Tracey

She does. They have just turned sixteen.

Mr Thomas

To lose your mother at such a young age is terrible. Is their father still around?

Tracey

It's a long story, but I'm sure he will be soon.

Mr Thomas

Keep me informed Mrs Green. It might be too late to help Miss Mason, but her sons I'm sure will need help at some point.

Brenda

Tracey love, I have just phoned Gary, he said he will bring them over tomorrow evening around six. He will bring his mate with him who will fit them.

Tracey

No problem, I'll be there.

A couple hours later, Halima accidentally knocks the peg off her nose.

Halima

(Frantically) Where's my peg? *(Looking for it, she realises that she is breathing fresh, clean air, shouting out)* Everyone fresh air has returned.

Everyone cheers as they take off their pegs

Tracey

I think this place is now ready for the arrival of a princess.

It's All In A Day's Work

Characters

Sheila Brown
A medium sized lady in her late sixties. She lost her husband many years ago. She has two children. Kevin, who is a teacher in London and Dawn, who still lives at home.

Doctor Sue
A tall woman in her mid thirties. She is bisexual.

Sizzling Sarah
A small woman in her mid sixties. She is on the large side, and has many tattooe. She does not keep her business clean.

Iris
A small woman who is ninety-four. She does get very forgetful.

Gary
A small man in his mid twenties. He is the youngest son of Brenda. He steals from houses to order. Despite this, he is very charming and has the gift of the gab.

Andy
A tall and good looking man in his late thirties. He is married, but shows no loyalty to his wife.

Other characters
Tracey, Bet, Lesley B, Brenda, Sandra, Halima, Sally, Miss Spears, Mr Thomas, James and Louie.

Settings
The factory, City Hospital, Sheila Browns house, Mandy's house.

It's All In A Day's Work

Sandra is hiding behind the factory bins.

Tracey
Sandra love are you alright?

Sandra
I would be if I could get these bloody handcuffs off.

Lesley B
Was it fetish night?

Sandra
It's the last time I trust a man. Five hours I was tied up on his bed and he didn't touch me once.

Tracey
Try five years in my case and if the man I married touched me I'd kill him.

Lesley B
What ever happened to love? *(They both laugh)*

Tracey
Well, you can't stay here with next to nothing on. Let's go and get her a coat from lost and found and give Brenda a shout, I'm sure she has something to get these handcuffs off.

Lesley rushes off and five minutes later she is seen walking alongside Brenda, carrying a coat.

Brenda
You and your role play, you kinky cow. What part were you playing this time?

Sandra

The heroine in King Kong. My knock off Kenny was dressed in a gorilla suit. He tied me up and said he would be back later when he had terrorised New York. As I lay there I thought Jack Prescolt, who was played by Jeff Bridges would rescue me and make me his.

Brenda

Who got to you first?

Sandra

His mother.

Tracey

Embarrassing or what?

Sandra

She said it was wash day and she needed the sheets. I asked where Kenny was. She said he had left a couple of hours ago to catch a flight to Ibiza.

Lesley B

Bloody hell.

Sandra

That's not the end of it.

Brenda

There's more?

Sandra

As I went downstairs there was another woman sitting at the kitchen table drinking tea. She asked which film I was in. I said King Kong, and she said hard luck love, I was Pussy Galore in Gold Finger, and believe me every part of my body was shaken.

Tracey

Let's hope next time you get to be in Diamonds are Forever. After last night you could do with a bit of sparkle in your life.

Lesley B

Who knows it could be a diamond in a ring.

Tracey

That's more than she would get from King Kong. *(They all laugh)*

Brenda

Right, leave her with me, I'll sort her out.

Sandra goes off with Brenda and Tracey and Lesley B walk into the factory. As Tracey sits down behind her machine, Miss Spears makes an announcement.

Miss Spears

As you know Mr Thomas has given over this morning to the making of baby clothes for baby Peggy. You can make any outfit as long as it can fit a child up to the age of five. The winner will be chosen by myself and Mr Thomas. You have got till eleven thirty, off you go.

Everyone rushes to the fabric cupboard. After twenty minutes they all make a start on their outfits.

Lesley B

Can I have your application form Sally love.

Sally

I'm not sure Lesley if I want to apply.

Lesley B

Stop taking the piss and give it to me.

Sally

But-

Lesley B

Tracey grab her bag.

Tracey quickly grabs Sally's bag and searching through it, she pulls out the application form. She passes it to Lesley. Lesley B takes the application and gives it to Miss Spears. Sandra walks onto the shop floor wearing a sarie.

Halima

What are you doing with my mum's sari on?

Sandra

I found it in the lost and found box and I have always wanted to try one on.

Halima

How does it feel?

Sandra

It feels so light and comfortable. I'm so glad I tried it on. I think I will keep it on for the rest of the day.

Tracey

(Whispering to Sandra) Is that the only thing she had?

Sandra

It was this or a pair of hot pants.

Tracey

That was a difficult decision. I wonder what King Kong would have suggested.

Sandra

I'll be suggesting something the next time I see King Kong. *(They both laugh)*

Miss Spears
Everyone, you have had two hours, you have thirty minutes left.

Sally
What a beautiful dress, she would look like a princess in that.

Tracey
My dress is for evening wear, your dungarees are for day wear. We should open a shop, we could become millionaires.

Sally
Tell you what, if we don't succeed in the next five years, we will open our own shop.

Tracey
That's a deal.

Miss Spears
Right everyone, stop your machines and put your outfits on your mannequins.

Mr Thomas appears with Miss Spears. They walk around the shop floor looking at each outfit. After a short time Mr Thomas announces the winner.

Mr Thomas
Thank you ladies. I can see why we are always voted best factory of the year. With such a high standard it has been a very hard decision to make. However every little girl wants to look like a princess so the winner is Mrs Green. *(Everyone claps)* Come and get your prize Mrs Green. *(Tracey walks over to where Mr Thomas is standing)* Well done Mrs Green. *(He passes her an envelope)*

Tracey
Thank you Mr Thomas.

Mr Thomas

As everyone has worked so hard this morning I'm giving you an extra half a hour for your lunch and a free burger from Sizzling Sarah. *(Everyone groans)* Off you go everyone.

Everyone walks to the canteen. Tracey walks with Lesley B.

Lesley B

Are we getting a burger?

Tracey

I know it's free, but with her food we will end up with some type of illness.

Lesley B

Think of how much weight we will lose when it rushes out both ends.

Tracey

I must admit I could do with loosing a couple of pounds.

Lesley B

Think how much money we will save by not joining Weight Watchers. We will be losing weight for free.

Tracey

Come on then. At least we won't have to queue.

Tracey and Lesley B walk outside to Sizzling Sarah's Burger Bar.

Sizzling Sarah

Frigging hell, here come the golden girls.

Lesley B

Hello Sarah love. Can we have a couple of burgers please?

Sizzling Sarah

Course you can. How do you like your burgers?

Lesley B

Very well done. *(Whispering to Tracey)* That way it will kill most of the germs.

Sizzling Sarah

Did you say something love?

Lesley B

I was just saying I bet it's hot in there, especially in this weather.

Sizzling Sarah

I'm bleeding roasting. I've got sweat running down me. I have to keep using my tea towel to dry myself off with and don't talk to be about the flies. I'm sick of bleeding swatting them. Look they are all over my kitchen units.

Tracey

Have you got a new tattoo?

Sizzling Sarah

Yeah, I got it done last week. It's the devil.

Lesley B

(Whispering to Tracey) Even he would have problem digesting her burgers.

Sizzling Sarah

What was that love?

Lesley B

I was saying it looks well done.

Sizzling Sarah

Our Briony's new bloke did it.

Tracey

Has she got a new bloke then?

Sizzling Sarah

She has. He is a right tosser. He has got several children by seven different women. He is always in and out of prison and he has never done a day's work in his life has he.

Tracey

So why haven't you told him to sling his hook?

Sizzling Sarah

Well I would do, but he gives me a discount when he does my tattoos. Even though he has put my Briony in hospital a couple of times, he always gets her a nice Gucci bag for when she comes out. He is not a bad lad. Good tattooists are hard to fine.

Tracey

You always was a good judge of character.

Sizzling Sarah

I've always prided myself on it. That's why when that tosser robbed my next door neighbour I kept my mouth shut as I want him to do a tattoo of Dracula above my lady bit. That way it will keep the men away from my bits.

Lesley B

(*Whispering to Tracey*) That's the last thing she needs with her sex life.

Sizzling Sarah

Did you say something love?

Lesley B

I was saying is it ready yet?

Sizzling Sarah
  (Lighting up a fag) Five minutes. Hope you don't mind, but I've made it a cheese burger due to the fact that my fridge packed up a few days ago and I need to get rid of the cheese before it goes off.

Lesley B
  You are so kind.

Sizzling Sarah
  Right here you are love. *(She passes Lesley B the burgers)* Do you want ketchup with that?

Lesley B
  (Looking at the flies around the open bottle) No, your food is just great as it is.

Sizzling Sarah
  You know where I am if you need a bit of quality food.

Tracey and Lesley B walks off and sit on the bench at the side of the factory.

Lesley B
  This burger better make me lose some weight.

Tracey
  Looking at Sarah's weight, good luck with that.

Lesley B
  With her under arm hair, she always reminds me of an East German shot putter.

Tracey
  Could do with putting one of those shots in a canon and blowing up her filthy van. It would help the environment.

Lesley B

That would save a lot of lives *(they both laugh)* what was your prize?

Tracey

A hundred pound book voucher.

Lesley B

That will come in handy.

Tracey

It was as though someone knew I was going to win.

Lesley B

I'm sure it was a coincidence. You taking Bet to the hospital this afternoon?

Tracey

I am, but I'm not looking forward to it. There is not much you can do when a doctor tells you your time is up.

Lesley B

For her two boys to be motherless at such an early age is heart-breaking. Any chance in locating the father?

Tracey

That's funny you should ask. I'm going to confront Bet about it. She won't like it, but the boys have a right to know. Look at the time I've got a taxi booked for half one. I better go.

Lesley B

I forgot to tell you.

Tracey

What?

Lesley B
Spearsey has agreed to look after Mandy and the baby.

Tracey
That's great news.

Lesley B
I think what sprung it was the chance for Spearsey to bring up a baby she lost all those years ago.

Tracey
Everything comes to those who wait. I'll see you on Monday.

Tracey walks to Bet's house, where she sees a taxi outside.

Taxi driver
A taxi for Bet?

Tracey
I'll just go and get her.

Tracey walks up Bet's path, just as Bet opens the door.

Bet
Don't worry I've not done a runner.

Tracey
You look a bit perkier.

Bet
With the time I've got left, I'm not going to waste it just feeling miserable.

They both get into the taxi and ten minutes later they arrive at the City Hospital. Paying the taxi driver, they walk into the cancer department and sit down in the waiting room. Five minutes later, a doctor comes out of her office and walks towards Bet.

Doctor Sue

Miss Mason?

Bet

That's me, but call me Bet love. Every young woman does.

Doctor Sue

You look a great bet to me. If I'm going to call you Bet, you must call me Sue. All the good looking woman do.

Tracey

It's like a dating agency. Bet will you be alright to go in alone?

Bet

I won't be alone. I've got Sue to take care of me. Please remember it's only Bet to the younger women, Miss Mason to those of a certain age.

Tracey

Bitch.

Doctor Sue and Bet walk off into the doctors office, leaving Tracey sitting on her own. Two minutes later, an old lady walks up to Tracey.

Iris

Excuse me love, you don't mind if I sit next to you?

Tracey

Not at all, sit yourself down.

Iris

Thank you love. I'm just waiting for my mother. She is in there with the consultant. It's not looking good.

Tracey

Is your mother still with us?

Iris

She is ninety-five, but was diagnosed with cancer two years ago.

Tracey

That's a shame.

Iris

It is, but she has had a good life. I'm Iris by the way.

Tracey

I'm Tracey.

Iris

Do you know Tracey, my mother was born into a loving family. She had two sisters and a brother, they were so happy growing up together. Even when they become adults they kept in close contact. When she was younger she travelled to many European countries and had such a busy social life. My grandfather had his own business so money wasn't a big issue for her. One night she went to the Palais night club and met her future husband my father.

Tracey

Do you know I met my husband at the same place.

Iris

How did it turn out for you?

Tracey

Not that good.

Iris

It was the same for my mother. Two sons and a daughter later my mother discovered what she had married.

Tracey
What did she discover?

Iris
His gambling, his unfaithful behaviour and his major drink problem, which resulted in row after row. He was always on the last bus and when he got home you knew it was time for bed as the alcohol would bring his nasty side out. How my mother survived, financially I'll never know. He was always dipping into her purse.

Tracey
Your father not with us any more?

Iris
The drink got him in the end.

Tracey
Sorry to hear that.

Iris
Don't be love. What goes around comes around.

A man in his forties walks towards Iris.

David
Sorry I'm late mum, the traffic was terrible.

Iris
That's alright love. This nice lady has been looking after me. Right come on then son, let's go home.

Tracey
(As they walk away) Are you not going to wait for your grandma?

David
My grandma died over twenty years ago, with my mother being

ninety-five. There's no chance of my grandma being alive.

They both walk away leave Tracey with her mouth open in disbe-lief. Bet comes out of the doctor's surgery and walks over to Tracey.

Bet
Come on girl, let's go.

Tracey
Everything alright?

Bet
Let's get back to my place. I could do with a large one.

Ten minutes later both bet and Tracey are sitting in Bet's garden drinking a large vodka.

Tracey
Was it as bad as we thought?

Bet
Worse. I was hoping for months, but with the cancer spreading to much of my body I've only got weeks. I don't want any tears, I've had a good life, so for that I must be grateful. My concern is for my boys and what is going to happen to them.

Tracey
While ever I'm here and all your other friends are, your boys will be taken care of. But I must ask you a question.

Bet
What?

Tracey
I think it's time their father comes into their lives.

Bet

Why should he? He has not had anything to do with them up until now.

Tracey

Seeing as he doesn't know they exist, there wasn't much chance of him playing a part of their life.

Bet

You know what I did to him.

Tracey

I do, but the boys have a right to know who their father is. Who was the friend he stayed with when he came to Nottingham?

Bet

Do we have to talk about this?

Tracey

We do, who was it?

Bet

If you must know it was Sheila Brown's lad.

Tracey

Do I know them?

Bet

Sheila Brown, she lives on Milverton. She has got a daughter called Dawn.

Tracey

Not Dawn who never comes in till dawn?

Bet

That's her.

Tracey

I've not see her for years and she only lives round the corner.

Bet

That's often the case.

Both twins walk into the garden.

James/Louie

Hello Aunty Tracey.

Tracey

Hello boys. Your mum needs to have a chat with you, so I will leave you to it. See you soon Bet love.

Bet

Thanks babe. *(They both hug)*

Leaving Bet's house, Tracey decides to walk to Sheila Brown's house. Ten minutes later she knocks on Sheila's door. Sheila opens the doors.

Sheila

Hello, can I help you?

Tracey

It's Tracey Green from Mildenhall.

Sheila

Bloody hell, I've not seen you for years.

Tracey

It's been too long.

They both walk into the hall.

Sheila

We will have to be quiet, Dawn didn't come in till dawn this morning.

Tracey

Has she not got a boyfriend?

Sheila

She did have, but he didn't match up to her first love Billy, so she ended it. Mind you, when it comes to Billy's manhood no-one can match up. I'll be glad when she gets back with him. She might get in at a decent time. Come into the living room and tell me what's brought you here.

Tracey

(Sitting down) I'm trying to find someone who visited here many years ago.

Sheila

Right.

Tracey

He was friends with your Kevin at university.

Sheila

Describe him.

Tracey

He must be around forty now. He was a medium sized guy with blonde hair and had a very beautiful face.

Sheila

Let me think. I know who you mean, Michael Steward, he made you have hot sweats by just looking at him.

Tracey

Are you still in contact with him?

Sheila

Not really, although he still sends me a card at Christmas. He has his own business in Cambridge. It's to do with computers. I hear it's a multi-million pound business. He did ask if my Kevin would go and work for him, but Kevin has always wanted to go into teaching.

Tracey

Did he ever get married.

Sheila

He did, but his wife tragically died in a car crash, she was six months pregnant at the time.

Tracey

That's terrible.

Sheila

It was. So horrible that he hasn't married again. Even though he did really want children.

Tracey

What is his company's name?

Sheila

Now you are asking me. Let me think. I know, Swift Creations.

Tracey

(Tracey looks at her watch) Bloody hell Sheila, look at the time, I've got to go.

Sheila

OK love. Pop round again when you have got the time.

Tracey

I will. Hopefully your Dawn will get back with Billy by then.

Sheila

We all live in hope.

Ten minutes later Tracey arrives at Mandy's gate.

Tracey

Sorry lads, have you been waiting long?

Gary

Just got here. This is my friend Andy.

Tracey

Hello. I'll just open the door. *(She opens the door)* Can you manage?

Gary

We will be fine.

Tracey

Great. I'm just going to pop round to mine, I'll be back in half a hour.

Andy

Can I pop round with you?

Tracey

Getting a bit fresh aren't you?

Andy

Who can blame me. It's rare to see so much beauty in one woman.

Tracey

Wife suffering from headaches is she?

Gary

Something like that?

Smiling, Tracey leaves Gary and Andy to fit both the fridge and the oven. After they have finished, they take a look at the garden.

Gary
What do you think mate?

Andy
Leave it with me. A couple of hundred should do it.

Tracey comes back and walks into the garden.

Tracey
What do you think?

Andy
A couple of hundred should do it.

Tracey
What about the oven and fridge-freezer?

Gary
Shall we say, three hundred, that way we will keep in your five hundred budget.

Tracey
I shall tell you mother what a honest caring son she has.

Gary
I like to think so. Right, I've got to go, there is a woman on Milverton who needs a three piece suite. I'm like a modern day Robin Hood, taking from the rich to give to the poor.

Tracey
It's a shame there is not more people like you.

Gary
Come on mate, let's go.

Andy

I'll pop round next week if that's alright. *(Not taking his eyes of Tracey for a second, he extends his arm to shake Tracey's hand)*

Tracey

(Shaking Andy's hand) That will be fine. *(Andy keeps hold of Tracey's hand until Gary grabs his arm to go)*

Gary

See you soon.

They both walk out of the door. When they have gone, Tracey with a smile on her face locks the door. As she walks up the hill, she feels a movement down below.

Life Changing

Characters

Ann

A medium sized woman in her late thirties. She comes from a working class background and is proud of it.

Christine

A black woman in her fifties. She has a very posh sounding voice and is dressed in designer clothes.

Julie

A small woman in her late thirties. She says it as it is.

Mr Steward

A very good looking man in his late thirties. He owns a multi-million pound business and is the father of Bet's children.

Veronica Wells

A tall slender woman in her early thirties. She is Mr Stewart's Personal Assistant.

Receptionist

A medium size woman who looks down on people.

Other characters

Tracey and Lesley B.

Settings

On the train, Swift Creations.

Life Changing

Both Tracey and Lesley B are on the train, heading for Cambridge.

Tracey

We would be just clocking on now. I can't believe you managed to get the day off for us and with full pay.

Lesley B

It was all about the timing of your phone call. If it had been a few minutes earlier, he would of said no, but when you called I had just positioned myself on top of him, which is his favourite position. He couldn't say anything but yes.

Tracey

What are you like woman.

Lesley B

You have got to have some perks when you are sleeping with the boss. But in fairness, as he knows about Bet's limited time, he wants to see her two boys are taken care of. So what do we know?

Tracey

We know he works and lives in Cambridge.

Lesley B

Did you say he has his own business?

Tracey

I did, it's called Swift Creations and by all accounts it's making a lot of money.

Lesley B

Rich and beautiful, I'm having an affair with the wrong guy. *(They both laugh)*

Tracey

Also he lost his wife and unborn child in a car accident.

Lesley B

That is sad. You can see why something like that would make him think twice about getting married again. But you did say he always wanted children. So that fairs well for our mission.

Tracey

Fingers crossed he doesn't throw us out of his office.

Lesley B

What with our hot figures *(they both laugh)* how are we getting on with your Samaritan work?

Tracey

Although I love it, it is very hard to work on the emotions.

Lesley B

I bet it is, some of the stories must be heart-wrenching.

Tracey

That's an understatement. I had a fourteen year-old girl on the phone the other week asking how she could keep her stepfather off her. I told her to speak to her mother about it. The girl said she had tried but the mother accused her of lying and slapped her around the face. She said she was desperate and she would run away if he carried on. I phoned the social services and explained it all to them. The next day they phoned me back to say that the step father had been arrested as he had done the same thing with children of other women he had been with.

Lesley B

Well done you.

Tracey

But the mother wouldn't accept it and threw the daughter out, telling her she was a jealous bitch who didn't want to see her mother being happy.

Lesley B

What happened to the girl?

Tracey

She was taken into care but as she explained, she could now take a shower and wash all of her body because she knew if she washed all of herself there was a greater chance of him walking in on her. They also told me that the dark circles around her eyes are fading because she can now go to bed and sleep, rather than being woken up in the middle of the night by the step father who wanted to read her a bedtime story.

Lesley B

How old was she?

Tracey

Fourteen.

Lesley B

Filthy perv. Just think Tracey Green, if you hadn't of volunteered, that girl might not be alive today, you have saved one and I know you are going to save many more. When does your access course start?

Tracey

Next week. I'm nervous but I know I'm doing the right thing,

Lesley B

Don't forget it.

Tracey

I've got a confession to make.

Lesley B
What have you done now?

Tracey
I've met someone.

Lesley B
Trace Green you tart.

Tracey
Nothing has happened.

Lesley B
(Singing) Tell me more, tell me more, did he get very far?

Tracey
Shut up you daft cow.

Lesley B
What's his name? Where did you meet?

Tracey
Well you know Brenda's youngest?

Lesley B
Gary, known as Robin of the Hood, yes?

Tracey
Well he came round with Mandy's new cooker and fridge-freezer yesterday and brought this guy called Andy with him to fit them. Also, being a jack of all trades, he took a look at the garden. Well as I shook his hand, his blue eyes just stared straight into me, which seemed to awaken me from a long sleep.

Lesley B
Snow White move over. Tracey Green has arrived.

Tracey

My body just came alive and down below was doing somersaults.

Lesley B

Are you ready for a man down below?

Tracey

I told them I was just popping home and would be back later.

Lesley B

So you ran?

Tracey

I had too, I was having hot sweats and palpitations. If I had stayed any longer I would have been dragging him up the stairs. When I went back to see how much it would all cost, he gave me his card and said ring me if you need any plumbing or bushes that need trimming.

Lesley B

Have you phoned him?

Tracey

I daren't, I know what is going to happen.

Lesley B

What's going to happen is you're going to enjoy being a woman again and letting your body experience what it was made for.

Tracey

But he is married.

Lesley B

So are you, in name. Go and have some fun girl, but don't forget to put yourself on the pill again, we don't want the patter of tiny feet.

Tracey

I'll think about it.

Lesley B

Don't think about it, do it. I went on a first date once.

Tracey

Did you?

Lesley B

I did, half way through the meal he took out a questionnaire form.

Tracey

He didn't.

Lesley B

He did. The first question was how many times would you expect to have sex with your partner in a week?

Tracey

Never.

Lesley B

It gets better. The next question was do you think if a woman is incapacitated to carry out her roles for example; headaches or tiredness, then a man should have the right to look for fulfilment with others.

Tracey

That's shocking.

Lesley B

The last question was, should a man have the right to expect a woman to give him a child every year for the first ten years of their marriage. Don't forget he wrote all of these questions himself.

Tracey

Did you slap him then leave?

Lesley B

I so wanted to punch him, but as it was a top restaurant, I waited for him to pay the bill. When we got to the taxi I said to him that I'm afraid I'm incapacitated at this time with a headache, so it would be best for you to look for fulfilment else where. I got into the taxi and told the taxi driver to drive me to the nearest club.

Tracey

Good for you. That showed the chauvinistic tosser whose boss.

A woman sitting in a seat at the side stands up and goes to sit on the opposite side of Tracey's table.

Ann

I'm not being nosey love, but I couldn't help hearing about the twat you went on your first date with. I had a disastrous first date also.

Lesley B

Did you love?

Ann

I did, we arranged to meet, like you did, at a top restaurant. I arrived first and felt way out of my comfort zone.

Tracey

Why was that?

Ann

Well, if I ever eat out, it's the local chippy at the bottom of my road. Anyway, the waiter sat me at my table and said if you need anything, let me know. Half a hour later my date arrives. He said he was sorry that he was late but he was having trouble with his ex-girlfriend. I asked are you? For the next hour and a half, he never shut up about her. He was saying how beautiful she is, and how she works around the world as a model. Then, for the next half a hour he talked about all the wonderful places they had been too. He finished off by telling me that she had an amazing fit body who likes to go to the gym every day.

Tracey

Nightmare.

Ann

He asked me if I did any type of exercise. I said I've just started running. Do you know what he said?

Lesley B

No?

Ann

Where do you run to? The chip shop?

Tracey

Shocking.

Ann

There's more. He asked where I was educated. I said at Cropt Comprehension. I live just down the road from the school. He said it must have been hell for me. I told him that I had lived here all my life, with all my friends and family around me, I said it is home to me. Do you know what he said?

Lesley B

What?

Ann

I bet that's what the people say who live in Beirut. Then he said are you able to cope when your friends and family are away for long periods of time at Her Majesties pleasure?

Tracey

I would have walked.

Ann

I waited until I had finished my food, at two hundred pounds a time, and finished my wine, which was eighty pounds a bottle and said I had to go to the ladies room. I walked straight past the toilet and straight out of the restaurant into a waiting taxi. As I looked back I could see my date brawling with the waiters. Two weeks later I saw one of the waiters in the club. He congratulated me on walking out. He told me that my date was usually the one who does the running, leaving his dates to pay the bill. As the police came and arrested him as he had no money to put the bill. His wife who had just started her shift at the local supermarket had to bail him out. She beat him with a stick when she got back to their council flat.

Lesley B

That was nice of the waiter to tell you.

Ann

So nice that we are getting married next year.

Lesley B

Good for you girl. What's your name?

Ann

Ann who gets the right man.

Lesley B

You certainly do.

Next minute a lady who had been sitting behind Tracey and Lesley B stands up and goes to sit on their table.

Christine

(In a posh voice) I couldn't help but hear your first date disasters, I had one as well.

Tracey

I'm Tracey, this is Lesley and this is Ann who gets the right man.

Christine

I'm Christine. I was talking to this guy on the phone for weeks. In the end we decided to meet up. When I got to the restaurant I was greeted by a guy who looked nothing like I thought he would of. He had tattoos on his face, up his neck, and love and hate tattooed on his fingers. I thought this is not my usual type, but I was in the mood for a bit of rough. We sat down at the table and halfway through the meal, I noticed a light flashing from his ankle. Next minute, several policemen came charging down the restaurant floor and pinned my date to the floor. Two minutes later, they carried him off. I asked the police woman who was standing near my table what was all that about? She said that he only had a two day pass from prison, and that was five days ago. I asked what he was in there for, and she said he was in there for beating up his last two girlfriends. I said that's funny you should say that as I noticed not only was he right handed, but on his fingers of his right hand he has the work hate tattooed on that. I said let's hope he can use his left hand when it comes to masturbating in prison. I said to the police woman do you know, with that many police coming to my rescue I feel as though I have got my money's worth from the council tax. Next minute the police woman said she's off duty, and do you mind if I join you, I've always been an open minded woman. We have been having an affair for the last six months.

Lesley B

Good for you

A woman walks up to the carriage.

Julie

I couldn't help but overhear, but I had an interesting first date.

Tracey

Did you love?

Julie

I did. I met this guy who as soon as we saw each other, he told me he had just come out as straight.

Tracey

That's different.

Julie

What's more he made me swear that I wouldn't tell anyone, especially if I met any of his family, as they wouldn't be able to cope with his new sexuality, and would probably throw him out. Also if I saw any of his work mates I was to keep it quiet as they would take the mickey out of him for being straight. I said, if being straight is so bad, why did you come out? He replied that he couldn't lie to himself any longer, especially when his body and his mind were telling him that he was straight.

Lesley B

Did it get as far as the bedroom?

Julie

It did, but I had to teach him what to do and where things went. It was hard getting him to stop taking me from the back, but after an hour we didn't go backwards again.

Ten minutes later the train driver announces that they are pulling into Cambridge station. Saying their goodbyes, they both get off the train and walking out of the station they get into a taxi.

Tracey

Can you take us to Swift Creations please?

Fifteen minutes later, the taxi pulls up outside Swift Creation. Paying the taxi driver, they stand outside the entrance.

Lesley B

Bloody hell girl, how big is this place? No wonder he is a millionaire.

They walk through the electronic doors and walk over to the reception desk.

Receptionist
Can I help you?

Tracey
Yes I hope so, we are here to see Mr Steward.

Receptionist
You mean Mr Steward the managing director?

Tracey
Yes, that's what I mean.

Receptionist
Have you got an appointment?

Tracey
No, unfortunately not.

Receptionist
Well in that case I'm afraid it will be impossible to see him today.

Tracey
Nothing is impossible, and he will see us. So stop looking down your nose at us and tell Mr Steward we have arrived.

Receptionist
(With a dirty look on her face, she makes a phone call) Mr Steward is in a meeting at the moment, but his Personal Assistant will be down shortly. If you would like to take a seat.

They both take a seat. Ten minutes later, Mr Steward's Personal Assistant walks over to them.

Veronica

Good morning. I'm Veronica Wells, Mr Steward's Personal Assistant, can I help you?

Tracey

I do hope so. We are here to see Mr Steward on an urgent matter.

Veronica

If you would like to leave me your message, I will make sure he gets it.

Tracey

It's of a personal nature.

Veronica

Well I'm his Personal Assistant, so your message will be safe with me.

Tracey

As I said, its a personal matter.

Veronica

I could call security?

Lesley B

You could, but when Mr Steward hears about what you have done, then I think you will find your P45 in the post. As Mrs Green has said, it is a very urgent matter, which will be life changing for Mr Steward.

Veronica

Would you ladies please follow me.

Veronica takes both Tracey and Lesley B up to Mr Steward's office.

Lesley B

(Whispering to Tracey) This office is nearly as big as my house.

Veronica

Could you wait here please.

She walks out of Michael Steward's office and goes into the board room where Mr Steward is having a meeting with several executive directors of other companies. She goes over to him.

Mr Steward

Not now Mrs Wells.

Veronica

It's very important Mr Steward.

Mr Steward

I said not now.

Veronica

I'm sorry Mr Steward but you are needed in your office.

Mr Steward

Are you telling me there is something more important than my meeting?

Veronica

Yes.

Mr Steward

Who is it that is in my office?

Veronica

There are two ladies waiting to see you. They say the information they have will be life changing for you.

Mr Steward

Have them thrown out Mrs Wells.

Veronica

No, I will not.

Mr Steward

(*Raising his voice*) I cannot believe how my Personal Assistant is acting. Gentlemen, would you please excuse me for a few minutes.

Mr Steward walks out of the boardroom and into his office. Veronica follows him.

Veronica

These are the two ladies who are waiting for you. Mrs Green and Miss Babbington.

Mr Steward

Ladies could you please tell me what is so important that I have to leave my meeting. You have two minutes before I throw you out.

Lesley B

You can see where the twins get their looks from. He is absolutely stunning.

Mr Steward

Thank you for the compliment, but you now had one minute left.

Lesley B:

You might want to sit down for Mr Stewart.

Mr Stewart

I'm fine where I am.

Tracey

Just over sixteen years ago, you came to stay at Sheila Brown's house, because you were very good friends with her son Kevin.

Mr Steward

It's a bit far back to remember but Kevin is still a good friend.

Tracey

When you stayed with the Brown's, you went out to the White Heart pub, and on all accounts you had too much to drink. In fact, you were quite drunk.

Mr Steward

Where is this going?

Tracey

Bare with me. Unbeknown to you there was a lady called Bet Mason sitting on the next table. You wouldn't have noticed in your state her staring at you, thinking you were the right person for what she had in mind.

Mr Steward

Are you making this up as you go along?

Tracey

I wish I was Mr Steward, do you want me to go on?

Mr Steward

Yes, do.

Tracey

At the end of the night you found yourself staggering back alone to the Brown's house, but on the way you were intercepted by Miss Mason and take into a wooded area where you had sex.

Mr Steward

Mrs Wells please leave us and tell security to go away. *(Veronica does this)* Although I was drunk, I still remember, trying to fight her off. But she was too strong.

Tracey

She was as strong as an ox in those days, so you never stood a chance.

Mr Steward

Even though I was drunk I know I was being raped.

Tracey

And you would have a very good reason to inform the police, but I'm afraid you are too late to go down that route, due to the fact that Miss Mason has terminal cancer and is expected to die in the next few weeks.

Mr Steward

That is sad, but what has this got to do with me?

Tracey

Miss Mason has twin boys Mr Steward.

Mr Steward

I'm sure their father will look after them.

Tracey

I hope he does, because that father is you.

Mr Steward

You what? I am their father? I don't think so. What she did to me I'm sure she did to others.

Tracey

Miss Mason is a lesbian Mr Steward. The thought of sex with a man disgusts her. But in order to get a child she had no choice. That is why she only did it the once. Here are some photos of the boys. As you can see, they are the splitting image of yourself. There is no doubt that they are yours. Now in a few weeks time the boys will be motherless and homeless, so will have to go into care. Is that what you want Mr Steward? *(Putting an envelope on Mr Steward's desk)* I have left you my address and phone number. If you are going to phone, don't leave it too long. Right Miss Babbington, we have a train to catch and we have exceeded our two minutes.

Both Tracey and Lesley B walk out of Mr Steward's office, leaving him staring at his sons' photos.

Lesley B

Do you think that gorgeous man will phone?

Tracey

Definitely. It doesn't matter how many millions you have in the bank. To see your child for the first time, no money can buy those feelings.

Animal Rights

Characters

Tracey, Sally, Lesley B, Miss Spears, Halima, Sandra, Brenda, Mr Thomas, Pop it in Pat, Dirty Mouth Deb, Gina Gin, Adrian Ache and lorry driver.

Settings

The factory.

Animal Rights

Tracey is at home, talking on the phone to Sally.

Tracey

They always say third time lucky, but as this is the third time in twenty minutes you have called me, who is getting the luck? I know you are nervous and you are having serious doubt about the interview, but keep thinking of all the strengths you will bring with you to the job. Strengths that Mr Thomas needs from a candidate like you. That's the only thing Mr Thomas is looking for. Although it would be wise for you to wear a short skirt and a see through blouse with at least two buttons undone. I know I said he will only be looking at your experience and strengths, but he is a bloke and when you get to his age he still needs to know that he is irresistible to women. What time is your interview? Then you have got plenty of time to search your wardrobe for the best outfit. Right, some of us have got to go to work, so I'll see you at ten.

Putting the phone down, Tracey leaves her house and walks down the hill. As she approaches Mandy's house, she sees Mandy and Miss Spears in the garden, with Miss Spears holding the baby.

Miss Spears

Good morning Mrs Green.

Tracey

Good morning Miss Spears. Good morning Mandy. How is the beautiful Peggy today?

Mandy

She slept right through the night, I was able to have my first of many showers and do a half an hour workout.

Tracey

I thought you were looking healthier. Keep it up. I'm sure your fairy god mothers appearance has made a big difference to your life.

Mandy

She has. I just hope she can help me find my prince now.

Tracey

(Looking at Mandy) Rome wasn't built in a day, it took many years to build. Talking about appearances are you planning on making an appearance at work today Miss Spears?

Miss Spears

What's the time?

Tracey

Twenty past seven.

Miss Spears

It can't be. I should have been at work twenty minutes ago.

Tracey

With Sally Docker going for the managers job this morning, it could mean if she gets it you will be having your pay docked. Carry on and it will be your P45 Miss Spears. *(Miss Spears smiles)*

Miss Spears

Come along Mrs Green and less of your lip or you will find yourself having a cold shower. *(They both smile)* Bye Mandy, I'll pop in later.

Tracey

(Walking down the hill) I think a new baby has put a spring in your step Miss Spears.

Miss Spears

It kind of replaces the one I lost all those years ago. Mrs Docker is still coming to the interview?

Tracey
After phoning me three times in twenty minutes this morning, she better be.

Miss Spears
I hope so. Between you and me, its her job to lose. I hope she dresses appropriately.

Tracey
Don't worry, she has been told. *(They both laugh)*

They both walk through the factory gates and head to the clocking on machine.

Miss Spears
The clock says you are five minutes late Mrs Green. We can't have that now can we Mrs Green?

Tracey
I think its fast Miss Spears.

Miss Spears
So do I Mrs Green. Pass me your clocking in card *(Tracey does this)* I'll put the right time on your card. *(She writes seven o'clock)* Have a good day Mrs Green.

Tracey
You too Miss Spears. *(Tracey goes and sits down behind her machine)*

Lesley B
Morning love. Have you heard anything from the Adonis?

Tracey
Funny enough I had a phone call from him last night. He would

like to come over next weekend.

Lesley B
What time?

Tracey
Around five.

Lesley B
If I'm not doing anything I'll pop round.

Tracey
You are like a dog on heat.

Lesley B
All us dogs like a bone between our teeth. *(They both laugh)*

Halima
(Walking past Tracey) Are you coming for breakfast?

Tracey
Is that the time? I think I'll have a full English.

Sandra
I had a full English last night. He cooked it just right. I was well done.

Tracey
The tart with the heart.

Sandra
It was more like jam roly-poly the way he kept rolling me around.

Tracey
Sandra love, it's half past eight in the morning, I've not woken up yet.

They all walk up the stairs and into the canteen. Tracey orders her breakfast. Brenda comes to the counter.

Brenda

I want a word with you young lady. I'll bring it over when it is ready.

Tracey

What have I done now? *(She walks over to one of the tables. Halima and Sandra comes over with their breakfasts.)*

Halima

How's college going?

Tracey

They explained yesterday what the course entails. The first term is with children, the second term is with the disabled and the third term will be with the elderly. I'm keep an open mind until the end of my course.

Sandra

I would have thought the elderly would be more suited to you due to the fact they are nearer your own age.

Tracey

You have never been popular have you Sandra love?

Sandra

Only in the bedroom.

Brenda comes over with Tracey's breakfast. She takes it to another table. Tracey walks over and sits down.

Tracey

Get your hands off my bacon. *(She slaps Brenda's hand)*

Brenda

Now then girl, have you got something to tell me?

Tracey

Not that I know of?

Brenda

I had a young man around my house last night.

Tracey

Lucky you.

Brenda

It would have been. But for two hours all he would talk about was you. I wouldn't have minded, but when I'm trying to watch Corrie and all I'm hearing is how beautiful you are and should I phone her to see if she wants to meet up for a drink, it's taking the piss.

Tracey

(Smiling) There's nothing going on.

Brenda

By the sounds of it, it's not the going on he wants but the coming off.

Tracey

Brenda, he is married and I am too, so there is nothing more to say.

Brenda

He feels much more, which he kept saying again and again right through EastEnders. Why don't you arrange to meet and tell him this? After all, if you had no feelings for him it won't be a long conversation.

Tracey

It's best we don't meet.

Brenda

So there are feelings there.

Tracey

With everything that is going on, it's best I stay away. Right it's time I got on. I'll see you later.

Brenda

This has got much further to run.

Tracey

I hope so. *(Tracey gives Brenda a kiss on the cheek)* Are you coming girls?

They all walk downstairs to their machines. As they sit down, Sally walks through the door.

Halima

Here she comes, the new manager to-be.

Sally

I've not had the interview yet.

Sandra

It's just a formality.

Tracey

The hardest part is when you get the job you'll have to manage this shower to do some work.

Sandra

(Looking at Halima) You will never manage that when there is food about.

Halima

You will never manage that when it comes to closing her legs.

Sandra

Piss off.

Halima

Tart.

Tracey

(Talking to Sally) I'm glad to see you have chosen the right clothes. If that skirt was any shorter it would be a waste of time. I said two buttons, undo one more. *(Sally does this)* Right, Spearsey is waving you over, good luck babe and don't fall down in that skirt, especially with these lecherous blokes around.

Sally walks off and goes into Mr Thomas' office.

Tracey

I hope she gets the job. She has gone through a lot over the last few years.

Halima

It will certainly give a boost to her self confidence.

Adrian

(Comes up to Tracey) Do you think I might stand a chance with Sally?

Tracey

I'll ask the girls. Girls do you think Adrian stands a chance with our Sally?

Sandra

Adrian love, with all that white stuff pouring from your face, it's not the part of the body a woman wants to see white stuff coming from. So the answer is no.

Adrian

Why do you women have to be so nasty to us blokes?

Sandra

Because you are blokes, now piss off.

As Adrian walks away, Sally comes out of Mr Thomas' office and walks over to Tracey.

Tracey

How was it?

Sally

Well I didn't think it went too bad, but there was a couple of questions that I struggled on. But I can't change anything now.

Tracey

What will be will be. Has he given you the rest of the day off?

Sally

He has. They are going to phone me later. So I think I will pour myself a large one and watch the afternoon film.

Tracey

You enjoy yourself love.

As Sally walks out the door, five minutes later Dirty Deb stops working.

Deb

(Talking to Gina Gin) These liners feel like real fur.

Gina Gin

Do you know Deb, I think you are right, and I've got two cats at home.

Deb

(Shouting Lesley B over) Lesley love, these fur liners are real fur and I for one am not touching them. Here you have a feel.

Lesley B

I must admit, they do feel like genuine article. Let me go and see Miss Spears. *(She walks into Miss Spears' office)* Miss Spears some of the workers are complaining that the fur liners they are putting in are real fur.

Miss Spears

What does it matter as long as they do the order and the customers are happy.

Lesley B

I'm afraid I have to disagree with you Miss Spears. No human being should ever have to handle a product that involves the killing of an animal, especially as so many animals are becoming endangered around the world. No-one has the right to bring about the extinction of one species so that another can show off their wealth. I demand that production to be halted until I've had a meeting with the workers to see how they feel about working with a material that can only be obtained through the slaughter of defenceless animals.

Miss Spears

This is a very lucrative order which is worth tens of thousands.

Lesley B

Sometimes there are more important things than money. I can see you are not prepared to stop production, so therefore I am calling a meeting in the canteen. *(She walks out of Miss Spears' office and standing at the front, Lesley B signals to everyone to stop their machines. Everyone does this)*

Tracey

Bloody hell, what is going on?

Lesley B

(Addressing everyone) There will be a meeting in the canteen in five minutes, I expect everyone to attend.

Lesley B walks up to the canteen, where she is followed by the workers.

Tracey

Lesley looks furious.

In the canteen, Lesley speaks to the workers.

Lesley B

I've called this meeting this morning because some of you might not know it, but for the last three hours you have been working on designer coats that have a real fur lining inside the pockets. I think this is disgusting and I want no part in it. Before I phone union head office, I need to know how you're feeling about this.

Dirty Deb

Knowing how they treat and kill the poor animals, it is shocking what management is wanting us to do.

Lesley B

Anyone else?

Pat

Out of all the profits the sellers make, I suspect they give nothing back to help animal charities out of the profit they make. Senior management should have told us about the sort of material we have been working with.

Lesley B

Listening to your opinions, are we all saying if senior management insists we must continue as before, then we will strike until our demands are met?

Everyone

Yes.

Lesley B

In that case, all in favour of strike action, raise your hand. *(Lesley B counts the hands)* All those who are not? *(No hands go up)* Then the motion is carried. I will now go back to senior management and see if they will agree to our terms.

Tracey

We'll have an early lunch before the strike kicks off.

Halima

As sure as night follows day.

After half an hour Lesley B comes back into the canteen.

Lesley B

Ladies and gentlemen. I have just had a meeting with senior management and they are not prepared to listen to any of our demands and speaking to the union head office, they are fully behind us in our actions. I have to tell you that from twelve o'clock today this factory is on strike. *(Everyone cheers)* I expect to see you all on the picket line first thing Monday morning.

Halima

So what does that mean?

Sandra

It means you can go home and stuff yourself with even more food.

Halima

What, like you can go home and act in your next film? Your insides must be made of cast iron.

Tracey

Ladies please. We are fighting senior management, not ourselves. Now the pair of you walk home together and you Sandra, make sure Halima doesn't go into any food shops on the way and you Halima, make sure Sandra doesn't talk to any men. Now off you both go. *(They both walk out together)*

Lesley B
What are you going to do?

Tracey
I'm going to catch up with my college work. What about yourself?

Lesley B
I'm going to spank the owner's bare bottom and tell him what a naughty boy he's been.

Tracey
You enjoy.

Lesley B
I will.

At around seven o'clock on Monday morning, Tracey is seen walking up the road to the factory gates. As she walks up, she can see a group of people outside the gate holding up banners. They are chanting '2,4,6,8, no more fur gets through this gate' followed by the singing of we will not be moved.

Tracey
(To Lesley B) I see the spanking didn't do much good?

Lesley B
I don't know. He couldn't sit down for hours afterwards.

Tracey
Why is Sandra walking bow legged?

Lesley B

She was playing Snow White last night.

Tracey

That woman loves her role play.

Mr Thomas drives up to the factory gate. Everyone crowds around his car waving their banners. As his car goes through the gate, eggs are thrown.

Halima

That will cost him a few quid to get his car cleaned.

Two minutes later a lorry comes up to the factory gate. The lorry driver rolls down his window.

Lesley B

(To the lorry driver) We are officially on strike and are asking you to not cross the picket line.

Lorry Driver

If I don't deliver these goods then I will lose my job. My kids will starve.

Sandra

(Walking over) Buffalo Bill you better not cross that picket line.

Lorry Driver

Bloody hell its Calamity Jane.

Sandra

If you ever want to feel my whip again you will do as you are told.

Lorry Driver

Yes Calamity.

With the sound of cheering, the lorry driver turns his lorry around. Everyone starts to sing the Deadwood Stage. (Whip crack away)

Lesley B

Right Tracey love, you have done your bit this morning, now get yourself off and get some of those essays written. This strike should go on for the rest of the week, so I don't want to see you till next Monday.

Tracey

But-

Lesley B

No but, be off with you.

Tracey walks down the road and before she turns the corner, she looks back to see everyone outside the factory gates and knows in less than a year, she will be walking out of those gates for the last time.

When One Door Shuts,
Another One Opens

Characters

Tracey, Barbra, Joan, Michael Steward, Bet, James, Louie, Lesley B, Pat, Sandra and ?

Settings

Bet's house, the factory, City Hospital, Tracey's house

When One Door Shuts,
Another One Opens

Tracey is hanging out her washing. Barbra Light walks into the garden.

Barbra
Morning Tracey

Tracey
Morning Barbra.

Barbra
How are you love?

Tracey
I'm bearing up with one thing and another.

Barbra
How's that beautiful daughter of yours getting on?

Tracey
She got there safely.

Barbra
I'm glad to hear it. Where is she living?

Tracey
Well for the first year she will be stopping in the halls of residence, although I'm sure she will become more familiar with the insides of a pub than her room.

Barbra
That's the life.

Tracey

I made sure that I sneaked a couple of condom packets into her suitcase.

Barbra

You are a thoughtful mother.

Tracey

You have got to be careful these days. Although, if the truth be known, its never quite the same with a rubber barrier.

Barbra

I agree. But when they take it off you don't want to be giving oral afterwards.

Tracey

The taste lingers in the mouth for hours afterwards. *(They both laugh)*

Joan comes out into her garden.

Barbra

Morning Joan.

Joan

Morning everyone. Have you heard?

Tracey

Heard what?

Joan

Mrs Walker has just given birth again.

Barbra

She's not?

Joan

She has. Her oldest is twenty-three.

Tracey

To see the bedroom as not just a place for sleeping in for many years, I do envy them.

Barbra

I agree. There's not many women who find their husband's still sexually irresistible after all those years of marriage.

Tracey

Your sheets are looking better Joan.

Joan

He has found himself a girlfriend. It's saving me a bloody fortune on washing powder.

Tracey

Let's hope he keeps her. Have you planted a couple of trees Barbra?

Barbra

Don't talk to me about those bloody trees. That daft man I married calls them two trees his orchard. I said to him what sort of apples do they produce, and he said 'large sweet apples.' I went to buy the same variety the other day, they were as sour as a lemon. I told him, come Bonfire Night you know where those trees are going, and he said 'they are my orchard.' Besides,' he said 'those apples aren't as sour as you.' So I get a dozen eggs and throw them at him. I said who's yoking now.

Tracey

(Laughing) Barbra, what are you like. Right I've got to go, I've got a young man visiting me in an hour.

Joan

Lucky you, who is it?

Tracey

The father of Bet's twins.

Joan

Good looking man?

Tracey

Let's just say a night with him would be heavenly.

Barbra

I'll have two's up when you have finished with him.

Joan

I'll have three's up.

Tracey

Anyone would think we were smoking a fag.

Tracey walks into her house and a hour later, there is a knock on her door. She opens it.

Mr Steward

Hello Mrs Green.

Tracey

Good afternoon Mr Steward, do come in. *(They both walk into the living room)* Would you care for some tea?

Mr Steward

Thank you, but I'm fine.

Tracey

I do have cups.

Mr Steward

I'm fine.

Tracey

Do sit down. *(They both sit)*

Mr Steward

I was raped Mrs Green. Although I had, had a lot to drink, I can still remember me trying to free myself from her grip. It haunted me for years after. So when you came to see me it brought all those terrible memories back. But I have two sons.

Tracey

You do. I can only condone what Bet Mason did and like all rape victims you deserve justice in a court of law. But I'm afraid you will never get your day in court Mr Steward. You must try and focus on the positives. You are a father of two beautiful, intelligent young lads, who I know, will do you proud. Knowing what happened to your wife and unborn child, God has given you a second chance to have the sons you so desperately want. I agree to get to this point, you have had to go through hell at times having to climb many a mountain to get where you are today. But remember the strength and determination you have shown has allowed you to be blessed amongst men.

Mr Steward

(Looking at Tracey with tears in his eyes) Thank you.

Tracey

You are very welcome. I know she did you very wrong, but when we go round to her house, remember she is a dying woman who is having to give her sons up to a man she only met the once over sixteen years ago. Unlike you, she will never see her sons graduate, get married, even have their own children. She will ask you not only to love and keep her boys safe but when they were born she put their names down to go to Cambridge University. She will ask you to honour that. The house will be passed to the boys which I'm sure you will sell, but will you divide the money between them and allow them to use it throughout their time at university. I know you are a very wealthy man, it will allow their mother to be a part of something she had dreamed of for many years.

Mr Steward
I will Mrs Green.

Tracey
Shall we go?

Mr Steward
Yes.

As they walk out of Tracey's gate, Lesley B drive past, blowing kisses at Mr Steward. Then they walk past Barbra and Joan's house, they are both waving out of their bedroom windows.

Tracey
Excuse the neighbours.

Ten minutes later, they arrive at Bet's house. Letting themselves in, they go into the living room where Bet, who is looking thin and very ill, is sitting. They both sit down.

Mr Steward
Hello Miss Mason.

Bet
(In a low voice) Hello Michael. You look even more beautiful now than you did sixteen years ago, and that's coming from a lesbian. I have very little strength left, so please allow me to speak. What I did to you all those years ago was a disgrace and all I can say is how sorry I am. I would have willingly gone to jail if I didn't have a body full of cancer. But they do say what goes around comes around and as you can see, it deservingly came for me. Although I hear you are a very wealthy man Michael, your money cannot buy the love and affection your sons need. Keep them safe and happy Michael, and tell them I will be with them in everything they do. Because I have such little

time left, will you take them to your house next weekend, so they can see where their new life is to be?

Mr Steward
I will. I will pick them up Friday morning.

Bet
That way I can say goodbye to all my friends without them getting any more upset than they are. I think I have just heard the boys come in, Tracey can you tell them I want to see them?

Tracey
You leave it to me, and I'll see you later.

Tracey leaves the living room and finds the boys in the garden.

Louie/James
Hello Aunty Tracey.

Tracey
Hello boys. Your mother wants to see you in the living room, she has someone to introduce to you.

The boys walk into the living room. Two minutes later, Tracey walks by the closed door, and hears Bet announce that Michael Steward is their father.
Monday morning comes, and Tracey walks to the factory gates. She is met by Lesley B.

Tracey
I see we are back in business.

Lesley B
I told you I would pad it out for the week.

Tracey
What swung it then?

Lesley B

I did, when I was swinging from his chandelier singing Dolly Parton's I will always love you. *(They both laugh)*

Tracey

What are you like.

Lesley B

How's Bel?

Tracey

Not well. I'm going to make an announcement at break time. On all accounts the twins are well pleased with their father. Louie was heard to say 'I've got the hottest father ever.' He couldn't take his eyes off him.

Lesley B

Can anyone?

Tracey

Come on girl. The sooner we start the quicker we will finish.

They both walk into the factory and clock on. As Tracey sits down, Mr Thomas comes out of his office to make an announcement.

Mr Thomas

Can I have your attention everyone. As you know the week before last we held interviews for the job of manager. We have had some very strong candidates, which made it very difficult for Miss Spears and myself. However, there was one candidate who shone through the most. Your new manager is Mrs Docker. She will be taking up her post from today. *(Everyone gives her a round of applause)*

Sandra

She can't be as bad as the last one.

Mr Thomas

Mrs Green, can you step into my office please?

Sandra

His voice sounded like Norman Bates in Psycho.

Tracey

Piss off you witch. *(Tracey walks into Mr Thomas' office)*

Mr Thomas

Sit down Mrs Green. I hope you are pleased with our choice of manager?

Tracey

I am. She just needs a chance Mr Thomas, and you have given her that chance. I know she won't let you down.

Mr Thomas

She better not. Although if the truth be known, there was only one person I wanted, a person who I know would have been fantastic. But unfortunately her life is leading her in another direction. But don't ever forget Mrs Green, you will always have a job waiting here for you. You are part of the family.

Tracey

Thank you Mr Thomas.

Mr Thomas

You are very welcome. Now, I hear Miss Mason is coming to her end?

Tracey

She is Mr Thomas. She will be lucky to reach the end of the month.

Mr Thomas

Is there anything I can do?

Tracey

Just pray that she goes peacefully.

Mr Thomas

I will. Do her boys need any financial help?

Tracey

They met their father the other day, and he is a wealthy man. So all their needs will be taken care of. Although when your mother dies no one can help with that need.

Mr Thomas

You're right Mrs Green. However, time does heal you enough to carry on. But there is not a day that goes by that you don't think about your mother when she has gone.

Tracey

If you don't mind I would like to make an announcement, that if anyone would like to see Bet and say their goodbyes, they can go this weekend. I hope you can make the time Mr Thomas.

Mr Thomas

I'm planning to go on Friday.

Tracey

She will like that. Can I ask you a question Mr Thomas?

Mr Thomas

Yes of course you can.

Tracey

Now, I know it is none of my business and what you do in your private life is nothing to do with me, but do you ever think you will make an honest woman of Miss Babbington?

Mr Thomas

You're right Mrs Green. It is none of your business.

Tracey

I only ask because Miss Babbington is such a wonderful person who loves you very much and doesn't deserve to play second fiddle to anyone.

Mr Thomas

I agree she is a wonderful person Mrs Green, but all I will say is my wife is in the advance stages of Parkinson's disease and not expected to be with us much longer. Is it not your break time Mrs Green?

Tracey

It is. Thank you for your help and support.

Tracey leaves Mr Thomas' office and goes up stairs for breakfast. As she sits down to eat, Pop it in Pat makes an announcement.

Pat

(To everyone) Could I have your attention please. Following 'fur-gate', it set me thinking that as a factory we should adopt our own charity, where we can raise money for a cause we have chose. I propose we should choose an animal that has become endangered, whether it be at home or abroad. I will leave a box on the side where you can write down the name of the animal then pop it in the box. The animal who gets the most votes will be the one we adopt. Please remember our children have the right to experience the animals that were around in our lifetime. You have until Friday to vote.

Tracey

Thank you Pat. I for one think it is a great idea. Talking of family, everyone here knows Bet Mason and you know she has not been well for some time now. Unfortunately, Bet's life is nearing its end. So if you want to see her and say your goodbyes, then could you please go and see her this weekend, as her time is very short. Thank you.

As they start to disperse, Brenda comes over for a word with Tracey.

Brenda

I know this is not the time love, but I can't help it any more. It's bad enough him going on about you when I'm trying to watch Corrie and EastEnders, but when he's doing it through Emmerdale, enough is enough. Just say you'll meet him?

Tracey

I will after Bet's funeral.

Brenda

Well that's a start. *(Tracey walks off)*

As the week progresses, Pop it in Pat discovers the extent to which her charity suggestion is taking off with her suggestion box being full. Also, Bet is seeing a lot of people coming by to say their good-byes. Friday morning comes, and Pop it in Pat talks to everyone who is on their morning break.

Pat

I would first like to thank you for taking the time to vote. The suggestion box was full. Counting all the votes, there are two clear winners. The first one was trees, although this is not an animal, I have included it. The other winner is the hedgehog. If anyone wants to join us in raising money for these two worthy causes then let me know. Thank you everyone.

Saturday evening and Tracey goes round to Bet's place where she finds an ashen faced woman who is skin and bone.

Tracey

Hello my darlings. I bet all these visitors have tired you out?

Bet

(In a low voice) I just about managed it. You did say the weekend?

Tracey

I did, but they couldn't wait.

Bet

Mr Thomas came to see me yesterday. He brought me some flowers and chocolates.

Tracey

That was kind of him

Bet

He said they all miss me and if there is anything I want, let him know.

Tracey

He might be the boss, but he does have a heart.

Bet

Before you go, I want to give you a little something.

Tracey

There's no need.

Bet

It's just a little something to help you through university. So you can buy some books and pay for a few bills while you are studying.

Tracey

I have not been accepted yet.

Bet

You will be my darling and you will work your ass off and achieve your dream. Now put that somewhere safe and don't open it until I've gone. It's been an exhausting day, so if you don't mind I'm off to bed. Night night my darling.

Tracey

Night Bet. I'll come and see you tomorrow. *(They both hug with Bet holding Tracey a little longer than usual)*

After a couple of minutes, Tracey turns and heads for the door. As Tracey turns and walks to the gate, a tear trickles down her cheek as something inside tells her it will be the last time she sees her dear friend. In the middle of the night, the phone begins to ring, waking Tracey up. She runs downstairs

Tracey

Hello?

James

(In a tearful voice) Hello Aunty Tracey. Mum was rushed to the hospital an hour ago.

Tracey

Which hospital my love?

James

City hospital. Can you come?

Tracey

I'm on my way, I'll be there shortly.

As she puts down the phone, she rings for a taxi. Dashing upstairs to change, George comes out of his bedroom.

George

What's going on at this time of night?

Tracey

Bet's been rushed into hospital. I've phoned a taxi, so expect me when you see me.

Ten minutes later, Tracey climbs into a taxi and soon after arrives at the City Hospital. Jumping out of the taxi, Tracey is seen running down the corridor to where James and Louie are. She finds them sitting in tears.

Tracey
Boys.

James
She has gone Aunty Tracey.

Tracey
I'm so sorry, come here both of you. *(They group hug)*

James
She started to cry out just after midnight. We went into her bedroom and saw she was in a lot of pain. She turned to us and said work hard and you will have great success. She said our father will take care of us now, so we didn't have to worry about a thing. She finished by saying to go and close the door, as her time had come.

Tracey
(Holding them both) Always remember what a great mother you had and where ever you are in the world, she will be with you. Now have you phoned your father?

James
No.

Tracey
Right, let's get you back to mine and we will phone him from there.

Twenty minutes later, they are all sitting around Tracey's kitchen table drinking coffee.

James
Will we have to leave our home?

Tracey

I'm afraid so. Your father live and works in Cambridge, so there's not much point of him relocating to here with his money, I can't see him wanting to live on a council estate. Although remember, just because someone has money, doesn't make them a better person. I would prefer a person to have a pure heart and be poor, than a rotten heart and be rich. You both would have been going to Cambridge to study anyway. Now when your father comes, he will take you home so you can pick up some of your clothes and belongings. Don't worry about the house, I will take care of everything this end.

Louie

You are very kind.

Tracey

Your mother meant a lot to me and many people on this estate. People round here look after one another. So if things don't work out you know where your family are. As you get older, your lives will get busier, but promise me every Christmas you will send me a card telling me what you have been up to.

James/Louie

We will.

Tracey

I think that's your father who has just pulled up.

Mr Steward

(Knocking on the door. Tracey goes and opens it) Hello Tracey.

Tracey

Hello Michael. Thank you for coming at short notice, the boys are all ready.

As the boys walk down the path, they turn and run back to give Tracey another hug. James pulls out a letter and gives it to Tracey.

James

Mum wanted me to give this to you.

Tracey

Thank you.

James

Bye Aunty Tracey.

As the boy get into their father's car and drives off, Tracey walks into the kitchen and sits down. She opens the letter.

Tracey

(Reading the letter) My dear Tracey. If you are reading this letter, then you know my life has come to an end. I didn't get to live all my life, but the time I did get I was blessed with so much happiness. So wipe away your tears and live life to the full. Now I don't want to worry you about the funeral arrangements as they have all been taken care of. Give my solicitor a call on the phone number I have enclosed. I chose her to deal with my affairs as she is the sort of woman I could have had an affair with. With they boys' father back in the picture, I didn't have to worry about their future, but, if you could try and keep in contact with them, even if it's just to remind them where they came from. I'm sure you will agree their working class roots were planted in the best soil. Two more things before I go. Because the boys won't want anything now, take whatever you want from the house or garden. There is a nice silver birch tree that would look very nice in your garden. I'll leave it up to you to decide where my ashes go. I know you will pick the best spot. Finally, my darling, it's time for you to open the letter I gave you. Thank you for helping to make my life so happy.

Yours as always

Bet xxx

Tracey goes to her coat pocket and pulls out Bet's letter. Openings it, Tracey finds there is a cheque inside for twenty thousand pounds, with a note saying 'do me proud.'

Tracey picks up the cheque and bursts into tears.

Welcome Home, Dear Friend

Characters

Janet
A medium sized woman in her mid-forties. She looks ten years older. She is the sister of Bet.

Other characters
Tracey, Lesley B, Adrian Ache, Maxi-Bates, Mrs Thomas, Brenda, Pop it in Pat, Miss Spears, Dirty mouth Deb, Gina Gin, The twins, Sandra and Halima.

Settings
The church, the Bull and Bush, the factory grounds.

Welcome Home, Dear Friend

Tracey and Lesley B are standing outside Emmanuel Church.

Lesley B

I know it's December, but it's bloody cold.

Tracey

They say we might get a white Christmas this year.

Lesley B

Are you doing much this Christmas?

Tracey

The usual. I'll be cooking the dinner, the old man will be reading Scrooge, and the kids will be falling out about what they want to watch on the telly. Then in the afternoon my mother will pull up wearing her Boney M costume and singing 'Mary's boy child' which is a bit far fetched, seeing as she has been a rocker for the first six months of the year and a punk for the second part of the year. My dad usually poles in a hour later, swaying and complaining about that there is no sport to watch. What about yourself?

Lesley B

Well I can't expect to spend the day with the man of my dreams because he'll be playing the loving husband and father role.

Tracey

Be round mine for twelve.

Lesley B

I couldn't possibly impose.

Tracey

Of course you couldn't. If I've got to put up with my kids and my parents, then so can you.

Lesley B
That's very kind of you.

Tracey
You won't be saying that when you are doing the washing up. *(They both laugh)*

Lesley B
Here comes the Adam's Family.

A coach stops outside the church gate, with many of the factory workers inside.

Tracey
It was Mr Thomas' idea to give everyone the day off and to supply the transport.

Lesley B
It was, although everyone would have attended the funeral anyway. So he didn't have much choice. But like most blokes they want to show everyone how great they are. It's the same when you ask them to clean up the house and they leave it until they hear you coming in. You find them huffing and puffing as he is doing the hoovering.

Tracey
Even if you came home at ten o'clock at night you would get the same performance.

Lesley B/Tracey
Men.

Adrian acne and Maxi-Bates walk up the church path.

Lesley B
Hello boys.

Adrian
She has left me.

Tracey
Who?

Adrian
The wife.

Tracey
What happened love?

Adrian
She said she was sick of washing my 1960's retro style clothes everyday and if she carried on doing it she would be singing Jail House Rock in prison because the only way to stop the pus from flowing was to chop my head off.

Lesley B
She has got a point. How many washing machines have you had this year?

Adrian
Our third one has just broken down.

Lesley B
Have you ever been to see a dermatologist?

Adrian
Is that something to do with animals?

Lesley B
That's a zoologist love.

Tracey

Leave it with me, we will book you an appointment.

Lesley B

Hello Maxi, I see you mum stitched gold threading around your pockets.

Maxi-Bates

That's for when it's night time so my hand can find my pockets. My mum doesn't want me to get cold hands.

Lesley B

Not much chance of that since your hands rarely leave your pockets.

They both walk inside the church. Next up the path is Dirty Mouth Deb and Gina Gin.

Deb

We knew this day was coming Tracey, but it doesn't make it any easier when the day arrives and her only in her fifties, I'm dreaming of getting that old.

Lesley B

Wasn't you a war baby Deb?

Deb

Cheeky cow. The only war I was ever in was with my old man when he came home pissed from the pub. The drink made him forget the times of the month when he could or could not.

Gina Gin

As much as we loved Bet, I wish she would have chosen a better time to go. I've still got some presents to buy and I've not even started to make my mince pies.

They both walk into the church. Next comes Pop it in Pat.

Pat

Morning ladies.

Tracey

Morning Pat. I had a thought the other day.

Pat

Steady on girl.

Tracey

In Bet's garden there is a silver birch tree that she was very fond of, I was wondering if we dug it up could we plant it in the nature garden next to the factory so we can put Bet's ashes underneath it? That way she would feel close to us and we to her.

Pat

That is a great idea.

Tracey

I thought we could have a whip round to get her a headstone.

Pat

Leave it with me, I'll sort it. *(She walks into the church)*

Mr Thomas and Miss Spears come up the path.

Mr Thomas

Good morning Mrs Green. Good morning Mrs Babbington. Even on a sad day like today you two look very radiant.

Tracey

You are too kind.

Lesley B

Isn't he. *(She shakes his hand and in doing so she secretly passes him a pair of jock underpants. Mr Thomas, looks briefly at what she has passed him and quickly goes into the church with Miss Spears following behind)*

Tracey
I would have thought he was more of a boxer man?

Lesley B
He was, but they didn't show off his hot ass so well.

Halima and Sandra are the next to come up the path.

Tracey
Hello you two.

Halima
Morning.

Tracey
What were you two arguing about?

Sandra
I was just saying it would be a good idea if Halima didn't go to the wake, especially as there is food there.

Halima
You are a vile witch. You know I'm on a diet.

Sandra
What is it? A seafood diet? See food and you eat it?

Lesley B
Ladies remember where you are.

Halima
Tell them where you were last night.

Tracey

(Looking and Sandra) Well?

Sandra

I was round a friend's house playing a part I'd always wanted to play.

Tracey

What part was that?

Sandra

The woman who gets attacked and eaten in Jaws.

Lesley B

How did that play out?

Sandra

Well, I filled the bath up with water and pretended to swim. Five minutes later, he comes in the bathroom wearing a shark outfit. As he attacks me he throws red paint over me to represent my blood. Next thing he takes off the arms from a shop dummy and throws them into the bath as my arms. But before he can do something with my legs there is a knock at the front door. He goes downstairs to see who it is and that was the last I saw of him. Apparently it was a loan shark at the door wanting his money. A body was found in the sea two hours later, of a man dressed as a shark. He went home to die. I left when the water got cold, but I'm still having problems getting this paint off of me.

Lesley B

You look like an Indian Squaw. *(Lesley B and Tracey put their hands over their mouths and make 'Red Indian' noises)*

Laughing, Sandra and Halima walk into the church and Brenda is the next up the path.

Brenda

Now you did say you were meeting at the weekend didn't you?

Tracey

I did.

Brenda

Because if I have to put up with it much more it wont be get out of my pub it will be get out of my house and my surname is not Mitchell.

Brenda walks into the church. Five minutes later a tall slender woman walks up the path. She stops in front of Tracey.

Janet

It's Tracey isn't it?

Tracey

It is, do we know each other?

Janet

I only know you from the letter Bet wrote to me. I'm Janet, Bet's sister.

Tracey

Hello, I didn't know she had any family?

Janet

She has two sisters and a brother.

Tracey

So why didn't she ever mention them?

Janet

Our parents, when they were still alive, were devote Christians, who when they found out about Bet's sexuality threw her out. All she had was the clothes she stood up in and no money in her pockets.

She lived on the streets for weeks until she got a place in a homeless shelter.

Tracey

Couldn't her sisters and brother help her?

Janet

We all wanted to help but our parents had threatened us that if we help Bet we would find ourselves on the streets as well. As we got older and left home, none of us had anything to do with our parents ever again. They died lonely, bitter people who were shunned by the rest of the family. We all regret not following Bet out onto the streets, but then we didn't have Bet's strength and determination.

Tracey

Don't be so hard on yourself.

Janet

It's hard when my brothers were being sexually abused by their father and then the next minute he turns around and condones Bet for being a lesbian, saying her sins had made her the scum of the earth. Let's hope the devil is ramming something up him so he is screaming for him to stop. *(She walks into the church)*

Lesley B

That's going to haunt her for the rest of her life.

Tracey

Here comes the hearse. I said I would walk in and sit with the boys, I'll see you later.

Giving the twins a big hug, Tracey goes between the twins and walks with them behind the coffin. They sit down on the front pews. From the pulpit, the vicar tells the life of Bet, up to her death. At the end of the service, the vicar asks everyone to think about Bet and what she meant to them. As everyone is doing that, the song 'I kissed a girl and I liked it' started to play, and laughter could be heard around the church. As the song finished, Tracey walks out of the church with the twins. Giving them both a big hug, the twins go down the path to their father. Tracey can be seen waving from the church door.

Two weeks later, Tracey walks into the Bull and Bush public hose. She walks over to where Andy is sitting, next to the open fire. He greets her with a kiss on the cheek.

Andy

What can I get for you?

Tracey

A glass of red would be nice. *(He orders a glass of red and brings it over to her)*

Andy

I see you found the pub alright then?

Tracey

I must confess, I had never heard of it before. It was my friend Lesley, who had been here on a couple of dates who had.

Andy

(Raising his glass) Here's to your friend Lesley.

Tracey

Andy, I'm not going to beat around the bush, but what are you expecting to happen between us both?

Andy

If I'm going to be honest with you, everything.

Tracey

Andy you are married, so am I. I have two children, you?

Andy

Two, by other women.

Tracey

So you just want us to turn our backs on our responsibilities and just run off together and live off thin air?

Andy

But when does it become our time?

Tracey

When we haven't got anyone who is dependant on us. Andy I have two children, one is nineteen and is at university, so as an adult she is old enough to stand on her own two feet. The other one is a fourteen year old boy who is my responsibility. I'm not going to walk out of his life and have him hate me for the rest of his. We have partners, which although it seems our marriages are dead, their feelings should be taken into consideration, due to the amount of time we have been with them.

Andy

So would you rather I walk away?

Tracey

It's not a case of you walking away but a case of us facing up to the situation we find ourselves in. Then there's us. For the next two years I'm going to be doing something I've wanted to do for years and that is to be a social worker. What do you want to do Andy? Because as I see it you go from job to job and do anything illegal on the side. I can't spend my life with a guy who bums around and goes from woman to woman having kids on the way but never taking responsibility for them.

Andy

You even twist the knife.

Tracey

It's not about twisting the knife, it's about being realistic. You may be a Jack of all trades, but I want you to be a master of one, with regular money. What trade could you be a master of?

Andy

I did go on an electrician course but I dropped out after six months.

Tracey

Don't tell me, the reason you dropped out was because of a woman?

Andy

Yes.

Tracey

Well the reason you are dropping right back in again is because of a woman. The right woman. Think about it Andy, in just two years I will be a qualified social worker, and you a qualified electrician. We could move to anywhere in the country with money in our pockets. I'm sick of being poor, having to buy second hand clothes and knock off furniture. If you want me, you now know what you have to do to get me. Right Lesley is hooting her horn. Thank you for the drink. *(She walks out of the pub and into Lesley's car)*

Lesley B

Everything alright love?

Tracey

It couldn't be better.

Friday morning comes and Tracey walks into the factory and clocks on. Before she sits down, Lesley B comes over to her.

Lesley B

Before you sit down, follow me.

Tracey follows Lesley B out of the factory and into the factory grounds. They walk up to Pop it in Pat.

Pat

What do you think?

Tracey

(Looking at the headstone under the silver birch tree) Pat, that looks beautiful. Such a fitting place for such a wonderful person.

Pat

With the money we have raised we are going to plant up the whole area, with trees and flowers and have running water.

Tracey

That will be peaceful.

Pat

It will be a good environment for the birds, bees and of course, the hedgehogs.

As they stand there looking at the headstone, Mr Thomas comes over with the rest of the workers.

Mr Thomas

Now that we have Bet Mason back where she belongs, I would just like to say a big thank you to all those people who have made it possible. I am so honoured to have Miss Mason in the grounds of my factory once again. As Mrs Macky and her team develop the site I for one will use it regularly. Along with the wildlife it will bring with it, this site will become a very special place. With Christmas just around the corner, I wish you all a very happy Christmas.

Everyone looks at Bet's headstone, and starts to sing Silent Night.

One Track Minds

Characters

Vera
A large size lesbian woman in her mid forties. She says it how it is in her dry sense of humour way.

Rita
A tall slim man in his early forties. He has been a transsexual for years and calls himself Rita.

Mrs Bates
A medium size woman who is the mother of Maxi. She is very dramatic in her quest to control every part of her son's life.

Other characters
Tracey, Lesley B, Sally, Miss Spears, Maxi-Bates, Doctor and Brenda.

Settings
Tracey's house, Queens Bower Road, in the ambulance, Queen's Medical Centre, the factory canteen.

One Track Minds

Sally is knocking on Tracey's door.

Tracey

(Shouting from the top of her stairs) If that's the bailiffs, everything is rented, if it's Sally, get yourself in here and put the kettle on.

Sally lets herself in and puts the kettle on. Tracey walks into the kitchen

Sally

Morning Mrs Green.

Tracey

Morning Mrs Docker. *(They both laugh)* I've not seen you for a bit. How's being a manager working out for you?

Sally

It's hard work, but do you know, I'm enjoying it. I do find the courses a bit boring at times, but they are helping me with my confidence. Although I don't think much of having to segregate myself from the workers.

Tracey

That is part and parcel of the job I'm afraid. You have to show the workers where the line is drawn and if that means you are unpopular, then so be it. Spearsey has been unpopular for years, but although she is disliked, she is respected at the same time. There are always those workers who will take advantage if they can.

Sally

How was Christmas?

Tracey
Christmas was much the same. We all went round to Joan's on Christmas night, Barbra's on Boxing Day and they all came round to us for New Year's Eve. A lot of eating and drinking, with a lot of laughs at the same time. Look at the time, we can't have the manager turning up late.

Putting their coats on, they rush outside the door. As they walk down Mildenhall Crescent, they see Miss Spears coming out of Mandy's house.

Sally
Good morning Miss Spears.

Miss Spears
Good morning ladies.

Tracey
How's Mandy and the baby?

Miss Spears
Mandy has had the flu but Peggy is fine. We all spent Christmas together.

As they walk down the hill to Queen's Bower Rod, they see a group of people standing in the middle of the road.

Sally
What's going on over there?

Miss Spears
It might be something to do with someone we know. *(They all rush over to see what's going on)*

Maxi-Bates
(Crying) A car went straight into me. He didn't even stop.

Tracey

You are going to be alright.

Maxi-Bates

I can't move my legs Tracey, don't let them chop them off.

Tracey

No-ones chopping anything off. Has anyone phoned for an ambulance?

Lady

Yes love, Reggie at number 33. He is off today, he is a butcher.

Maxi-Bates

That's a sign they are going to chop my legs off. They will sell the meat on my legs for a pound a pound.

Tracey

Your legs are only bone and gristle, so they will only sell for half the price. *(Everyone in the crowd laughs)*

Sally

They wouldn't call you Florence Nightingale, more like Doctor Crippen.

Miss Spears

At least it has lightened the mood.

Tracey

Here comes the ambulance. Shall I go with him?

Miss Spears

You have got work to do.

Sally

As the manager, that will be fine Mrs Green. I'll get Lesley to phone his mum. You head back when she gets there.

Tracey
Will do.

The ambulance women rush over.

Rita
Now then young man, what has been going on here?

Maxi-Bates
A car hit me. They won't chop off my legs and sell them for meat will they?

Rita
You will be lucky to get a snack out of those legs.

Vera
Believe me, I've thrown much better away.

Rita
Well you would you've been a lesbian for years. *(Everyone laughs)* Right let's get you into the ambulance, and if you are lucky we will put the blue flashing lights on *(looking at Vera)* or should that be a red flashing light?

Maxi-Bates
Don't you put that on if it's an emergency?

Vera
That's right, I've been dying for a piss for the last two hours.

They put Max on a stretcher and lift him into the ambulance. Tracey follows behind. Vera goes off to drive and Rita stays in the back of the ambulance. The ambulance speeds off towards Queen's Medical Centre.

Tracey

So Maxi what happened?

Maxi-Bates

Well, I was walking behind couple of girls who work in the canteen. My hands got cold so I put them in my pockets to keep them warm.

Tracey

Of course you did.

Maxi-Bates

But then I realized that I was wearing the trousers that my mother hadn't finished sewing the trouser pockets, so there was some loose threads hanging. My nails got caught in the threads which made me take my eyes off the road for just a second.

Tracey

That's when the car went into you?

Maxi-Bates

That's right, and didn't stop.

Tracey

I'm sure the police will be very interested to speak to you, so make sure you remember everything.

While Tracey is talking to Maxi, she notices he can't take his eyes off Rita.

Rita

It's good to see your middle leg is still working.

Tracey

(To Rita) Have you been a transsexual for long?

Rita

About ten years now. *(Maxi can be seen with his mouth open in disbelief)*

Tracey

Have you found love yet?

Rita

I wish. All I ever end up with is dirty old men who have never heard of soap and who don't even use anything to secure their dentures. The last guy I was with I didn't know whether to fuck it or harpoon it.

Tracey

Well, you keep trying girl. One of those frogs, will turn into a prince one day.

Rita

I won't hold my breath.

The ambulance arrives at the hospital. Vera comes round to the back and pushes the trolley into the hospital.

Vera

Best that you go and sit in the waiting room love. With his high sexual appetite the fewer woman around the best.

Tracey goes to sit in the waiting room. Ten minutes later, Lesley B walks in.

Tracey

Bloody hell what are you doing here?

Lesley B

As the trade union rep, it's my duty to see that all my members are fit and well.

Tracey
So in other words you wanted a morning off.

Lesley B
I did. There is only so many buttons you can put onto a woman's jacket. I started to think I'm getting paid buttons, so why should I sit here and sew buttons.

Tracey
What you do for love.

Lesley B
Talking of love, his wife died last night.

Tracey
That is sad.

Lesley B
It was, seeing as he was in my bed at the time he took the phone call. There is nothing worse when you are half-way through something and you have to stop.

Tracey
I bet it left you frustrated?

Lesley B
Frustrated is not the word. My body was mortified. It went from pleasure to despair in six seconds.

Tracey
So he's going to be off for sometime then?

Lesley B
I think a couple of weeks. But if he thinks I'm going without it for a couple of weeks he is very much mistaken. Docker is in charge.

Tracey

Is she ready for the responsibility?

Lesley B

She is either going to sink or swim. I've got the arm bands ready just in case. Talking of sinking and swimming, don't you start your work placement?

Tracey

Special needs.

Lesley B

Half of the people working in the factory are special needs, so you should fly through it. Talking of special needs, here comes Mrs Bates.

Mrs Bates

Where is he? Where is my baby boy? *(She is in floods of tears)*

Tracey

He is going to be alright Mrs Bates. I'm sure it's not serious.

Mrs Bates

(Wailing on the floor) What if he's dead? I can't go on without my little Maxi. It is all because I didn't finish the pockets on his new work trousers.

Lesley B

Why didn't you?

Tracey

This is not helping.

Mrs Bates

Why? I'll tell you why. I had a sherry while I was watching Midsomer Murders. It helps me steady my nerves while the murders are being committed. There was only ten minutes left till the end, but I fell asleep, which meant I didn't get to finish the pockets. Also I didn't get to find out who the murderer was.

Lesley B

It was the milkman.

Mrs Bates

Was it?

Lesley B

Yes, because each victim only wanted one pint instead of two, so there was not enough money for him to cream off the top.

Mrs Bates

I thought it might be him.

Tracey

(Looking at Lesley and shaking her head) Come and sit on a chair Mrs Bates, the doctor is coming over.

Doctor

Are you with Max Bates?

Tracey

We are, this is his mother.

Doctor

Well, he has broken his right leg, but there is only bruising on his left leg, so he has gone to the plaster room to have his leg put into plaster.

Lesley B

That's a bit like you Mrs Bates, getting plastered last night,

Mrs Bates

I only had the one. Do you think I have a drink problem?

Tracey

Of course not. You are a loving mother.

Lesley B

And grandmother.

Mrs Bates

Grandmother?

Lesley B

One day you will be a loving grandmother as well.

Mrs Bates

I hope so. Although, I will make sure I get to choose the right girl for my Maxi. I don't want him touching any old tart. I want Max to lose his virginity with a decent girl who he can respect. No slapper will get near my Maxi.

Doctor

Would you like to follow me Mrs Bates and I'll take you to see your son.

Tracey

You will fall in your own mouth one of these days, it's big enough.

Lesley B

The way she goes on is enough to put you off children for life. The least thing that goes off, she is looking for an Oscar. No wonder Maxi's hands are always in his pockets when he's got a controlling mother like that. Changing the subject, as you have only got a few months left why don't we have a night out?

Tracey

I could do with a night out. All I seem to do is work, work and work.

Lesley B

Right I'll sort it out. I'll get some of the girls together. Bingo and a club should do it. We will call it Tracey's last stand.

Tracey

Why have I got the feeling that the morning after the night before I won't remember a bloody thing?

Lesley B

Let's do it at Easter. You will get crucified at night and when the hangover has lifted it will be a 'new life.'

Tracey

Have you gone religious?

Lesley B

Not with my sinful life. When you are in bed with your lover and he gets a phone call to say his wife has died I won't be bathing in Holy water any time soon.

Tracey

It's a good job, because all water is bound to change to acid. *(They both laugh)*

Lesley B

Right girl, if we go now we will make it back in time for lunch.

Both Tracey and Lesley B head back to work.

Tracey

Have you looked at Adrian Acne's face recently?

Lesley B

I try not to if I can help it.

Tracey

The next time you see him, have a close look at his face. The dermatologist we booked him in to see has really made a difference.

Lesley B

You mean you can find his face in a snow drift now?

Tracey

You can. But whether you would want to pull him out of it, is another matter. *(They both laugh)* Rumour has it he asked Sally Docker out for a drink and she said yes.

Lesley B

She must have ran out of batteries, that will teach her to stock up.

Tracey

You are becoming a bitter woman Lesley Babbington. Is Sandra your new trainer?

Lesley B

Sandra? She's Gone with the Wind. I'm more of the Lion King myself.

Tracey

Is that on account you like your meat fresh?

Lesley B

As fresh as it is able at my age. *(Walking into the factory)* Right, I better go and see how Docker is getting on. If she has made any mistakes with her size boots, they are bound to be big ones.

Tracey

I'm off to the canteen for lunch. I'll see you later.

Tracey gets her lunch and sits down at a table. Brenda comes and sits next to her.

Brenda

Well girl, you don't hold back.

Tracey

If we are talking about Andy, then I only told him what I expect from a partner.

Brenda

So I heard. When he came round the next day, luckily Corrie wasn't on due to England's qualifying game for the World Cup. So he has got to wait for two years and go to college.

Tracey

As I said to him, while my son is still at school, I have a responsibility to him. Brenda, I want a man who has a trade behind him. Someone who can bring in regular money. I'm sick of being skint.

Brenda

I know where you are coming from. But the problem is, he is a bloke. There is no way he is going to go without his oats for two years. You will be lucky if he can last for two days.

Tracey

So he hasn't enrolled onto an electrician course then?

Brenda

The only thing he has enrolled on is a lads' holiday to Ibiza and I shouldn't say, but he's got a couple of new women on the go who are bisexual. They invite him round for a threesome at least once a week. I must get back, see you later.

Brenda goes back around the counter, leaving Tracey staring at the wall with a tear in her eye.

Tracey's Last Stand

Characters

Stevie

The Bingo caller. He is a short, plump man in his mid twenties. He thinks he is god's gift to women. He uses his job to get his leg over.

Karen

She is a medium sized woman in her mid thirties. She is an attractive woman who likes to explore her bisexuality with her partner, Julie.

Julie

A tall slim woman in her mid twenties. She likes to be adventurous in the bedroom.

Bouncer

A tall fit man in his thirties.

Lucy

A short woman who says it how it is. She is the manager of the Bingo hall.

Other characters

Tracey, Lesley B Halima, Sandra, Brenda, Deb, Andy, Mr Thomas, Sally and the police officer.

Settings

Tracey's house, Bingo Hall, NG69, Chip shop, police cells.

Tracey's Last Stand

Lesley B and Sally knock on Tracey's door.

Tracey
(Shouting from the top of her stairs) If it's burglars, don't touch me capodimonte, if it's a couple of tarts looking for a good time, get yourself in here and pour yourself a large one.

Lesley B and Sally go straight into the kitchen and pour themselves a large gin. Tracey comes downstairs.

Lesley B
Bloody hell girl how tight is that dress?

Sally
Have you had a boob job? They look amazing.

Tracey
They are natural.

Lesley B
You are seriously going to get some male attention tonight.

Tracey
The amount of gin you have got in that glass, you won't know what day it is, never mind whose trying to get you into bed.

Lesley B
Well, the amount of times I've seen my lover since his wife died, I may as well see someone else.

Tracey
Stop it now, what with the funeral and having to be there for his children.

Lesley B

What about him being there for me? I'm the best tonic for him.

Tracey

Talking of tonic did you put any in your glass?

Lesley B

I'm having it neat like my men. *(They all laugh)*

There is a knock on the door.

Sally

They have come back for the capodimonte.

Tracey

(Opening the door) Here they are, the seafood dieter and the Nightmare on Elm Street.

Sandra

Hello Tracey love. The girls are back in town.

Lesley B

(In the kitchen) Good evening girls.

Halima

Hello everyone.

Lesley B

Here you go girls, get that down you *(she passes them two glasses of gin)* have you been off this week Sandra?

Sandra

I have.

Tracey

Did you go anywhere nice?

Sandra
I went to the Oscar's in Hollywood.

Lesley B
What film were you nominated for?

Sandra
The Wizard of Oz, the Revenge.

Lesley B
How did that go?

Sandra
I played Dorothy.

Lesley B
I thought Dorothy was played by a sweet and innocent person who still has her virginity?

Sandra
That's where the revenge part comes into it as Dorothy is played by a mad, sex-crazed beast who is even feared by the Wicked Witch of the West. So much so that when Dorothy catches up with her, the witch wets herself and the water makes her melt away. As for the Munchkin Men, Dorothy has to have four at a time, as four quarters make a whole one.

Lesley B
So did you win?

Sandra
I did. In my acceptance speech, I thanked all of you for giving me the chance and experience to be the great actress I am today.

Tracey
How did we help?

Sandra

You, Tracey love, taught me how to play frigid roles.

Tracey

Bitch.

Sandra

You Lesley, have taught me how to play a mistress, especially in historical films like Henry VIII and his six and a half wives.

Lesley B

Cow.

Sandra

You Halima are always there to remind me what over-eating can do to a person.

Halima

Slapper. Your next film should be Halloween because you are a scary bitch.

Sandra

Do you know Halima, I think you are onto something there. The Bride of Dracula. I feel another Oscar coming my way. *(They all laugh)*

There is a knock at the door.

Tracey

(Opening the door) Here comes Baby Jane and Blaunch.

Deb

Piss off granny and shift out of the way, I need a drink. *(She rushes in)*

Tracey

Hello Brenda love.

Brenda

You look a million dollars in the outfit. If a certain man could see you now, he would be begging for you to forgive him *(They both walk into the kitchen)* You see Halima, that is the sort of figure you'll start to get when you stick to a diet.

Tracey

No Gina tonight?

Deb

No. She is staying in to wash her hair. The hair under her arms. *(Everyone laughs)*

Lesley B

Apologies from Pop it in Pat, she said she has popped it in enough, especially as half the fun of going out is getting it off.

Tracey

Chance would be a fine thing.

Sandra

Where is your husband tonight?

Tracey

He has joined a book club.

Deb

You should join as well, especially if they are reading The Joys of Sex, it might jog your memory girl. *(They all laugh)* This is a good bit of gin, where did you get it from?

Tracey

Brenda's Gary got it.

Brenda

It's his new line.

Deb

It's a good job he is always crossing the line. Tell him to get me a couple of bottles. I'll pay you next week.

Lesley B

Now before we go. I want to propose a couple of toasts. First to a person who is a great friend to everyone. Now, I know you are not leaving us yet, but when you do, remember you may be leaving the factory, but you will never leave our hearts. Tracey Green everyone. *(Everyone raises their glass)* The second is a toast for our dear friend who cannot be here with us any more. But, if she was, we know she would have been with us tonight. You will always be in our hearts. Raise your glass to the wonderful Bet. *(They all raise their glasses)*

Brenda

Taxi is here.

They all pile into the taxi and twenty minutes later, they are outside the bingo hall. They all walk in and find a table to sit at.

Lesley B

Are we sharing the winnings or are we being greedy gits and the winner keeps it all?

Tracey

Well if you say it like that we'd all better share it.

Halima

It's good to share.

Sandra

Until it comes to sharing food.

Halima

Do you ever share your film roles?

Sandra

I perform too well to share.

Halima

That's because one size fits all. *(They all laugh)*

Stevie

Good evening ladies, I'm your bingo caller Stevie. Who's feeling lucky tonight? *(Everyone shouts yes)* And if you're feeling really lucky, I could be your icing on the cake.

Lesley B

What sort of cake is it?

Deb

It must be Battenburg, because I would batter him if he came anywhere near me. *(They all laugh)*

Stevie

I'm more Victorian sandwich, as I like to be in the middle of two women at a time.

Brenda

(Shouting) Woman could get hung in Victorian times, but she wouldn't get hung with your weeny. *(They all laugh)*

Stevie

Right ladies, we are going for the four corners. North, South, East and West. Doggy style is the best.

Halima

This guy is barking.

Sandra

His looks are rough too.

Stevie

Number 24, I'll be outside your bedroom door. Number 32, I'm walking in your bedroom to you. Number 64, I'm on my knees and more. Number 38, I'm giving it you on a plate.

Tracey

Who is this twat?

Sandra

Bingo.

Stevie

We have got our first winner for tonight. Seventy pounds to you young lady.

Brenda

Young lady? This guy is full of it.

Stevie

We are now playing for a full line in the middle. Number 21, just my age. *(Everyone in the hall laughs)*

Deb

He has had a hard life.

Stevie

Number 76, I'll be free tomorrow at six. Number 59, then I'm free at nine. Number 7, I'll be free at eleven.

Brenda

Bingo.

Stevie

We have another winning lady, who is taking home seven

hundred pounds.

Sally

(Singing) Luck be a lady tonight.

Stevie

Right ladies, it's the biggy now and money as well. *(Everyone in the room raises their hand and gestures with it)*

Deb

(Shouting) There's not much point in doing that ladies, he's got nothing to put in it.

Stevie

(Looking embarrassed) Number 69, the witches are alive. Number 79, the witches have arrived. *(Everyone shouts tosser)* Unlucky for some, number 13.

Deb

It's not unlucky for me, bingo. *(Everyone claps)*

Stevie

Seven-thousand pounds.

Halima

That's one thousands, one hundred and ten for each of us. *(Everyone on the table starts singing We Are The Champions)*

When Stevie has finished his shift, he goes to see the manager in her office.

Stevie

Did you want to see me?

Lucy

Only as long as I need to.

Stevie

What's that supposed to mean?

Lucy

I have never known a guy to love himself so much. This bingo hall is not a place for you to advertise for sex.

Stevie

I was only having a laugh with the punters.

Lucy

It was a shame they weren't laughing with you rather than at you. When everyone, and I mean everyone, puts their hand in the air to show you what they thought of you, your response was to call them witches. Well, keeping with the theme, the response from this witch is to give you your p45.

Stevie

You're joking aren't you?

Lucy

One thing about witches, they never joke. *(Lucy puts her hand up and gestures with it.)* Get out. *(With his head down, Stevie leaves the office)*

After another hour, they all decide to go clubbing. On the way, they walk past a restaurant window.

Brenda

Here everyone, is that Mr Thomas?

Deb

So it is. Look, he has got a woman with him.

Lesley B

(Staggering to the window) What was that you said? *(She takes a*

look through the window) I don't frigging believe it. I'm going to have that bitch, thinking she can take my man. *(Rushing in the restaurant, she goes up to Mr Thomas)* So you think you can take my man you filthy tart. Well let me tell you no slut is taking my man away.

Mr Thomas

Lesley shut up.

Lesley B

Don't tell me to shut up you two-timing git. For years, I've had to play the other woman. I didn't want to, but because I loved you, I put up with it and now that your wife has gone you think you can cheat on me with that slapper. *(The other women all rush in)*

Tracey

(Putting her arms around Lesley, she moves her to the door) Come on love, let's get you away from him.

Lesley B

How can he do this to me when I love him so much. *(Tracey takes Lesley outside)*

Deb

(To Mr Thomas) You're despicable.

Brenda

You're disgusting.

Sally

(Shakes her head) Shocking.

Halima

How could you?

Sandra

Robin Hood would never do that to Maid Marion!

After they all made their point, they leave the restaurant.

Tracey

(To Lesley B) Come on I'll take you home.

Lesley B

Home? Are you taking the piss? I'm a single woman now. I'll show him what it's like to be cheated on. It's time to find a man or two. Where are we going?

Tracey

NG69.

Deb

I don't think anyone in there will be satisfying you tonight. *(They all laugh)*

Lesley B

I'm going lesbian.

They all walk to the door of the club.

Bouncer

Sorry ladies, but there are too many women wanting to come in at the same time.

Sandra

(Walking up to the bouncer) What did you say?

Bouncer

Evening Sandra, I didn't see you there.

Sandra

If it wasn't for me you wouldn't be standing there now.

Bouncer

You are all welcome.

They all walk in and go straight to the bar.

Tracey

How did you manage that?

Sandra

We were on the Titanic together. As he was sinking I pulled him out of the freezing water and on to my life boat.

Tracey

That was brave of you.

Sandra

Not really. He is hung like a donkey, even the freezing water made no impact on his size. Although his mate sank without a trace.

Deb

Isn't that the bingo caller?

Brenda

It is. He looks pissed.

Deb

(A guy dressed in leather with a big moustache and leather cap is talking to Stevie) By the looks of it he is going to get fucked twice in one night. *(They all laugh)*

Tracey

I'm off to the toilet.

Lesley BL

I'm off for a dance. Come on girls.

Tracey walks to the toilet. As she walks through to the washroom, Andy walks towards her.

Andy

Hello.

Tracey

Gay clubs now is it?

Andy

A couple of women friends are bisexual, so they like to come in here and check out the talent.

Tracey

Like they checked you out you mean?

Andy

I'm sorry about that. I don't know what came over me. You look great tonight.

Tracey

The only thing that came over you was two naked women. Thanks for the compliment. Try and keep my look in your mind so you can always remember what you could have had, every day of your life.

Andy

Please forgive me.

Tracey

No.

Bouncer

(Walking into the washroom) Everything alright love?

Tracey

Everything is just fine now. *(Tracey walks into the toilet)*

Bouncer

That is one hot woman. To wake up to her every morning would be a dream come true. *(The bouncer walks away)*

Andy slides down the wall, crying uncontrollably on the floor.

Andy

(*Shouting*) I love you so much, please forgive me!

Tracey

(*Coming out of the toilet, she washes her hands*) No. (*She walks to the dance floor*)

Sally

These gay guys can really dance. They put John Travolta in the shade.

Lesley B

That transvestite's make-up is amazing.

Brenda

(*Coming back from the toilet*) I'm glad I'm not a bloke, they are queuing for the toilet.

Gay Mark

It's gone one o'clock love, the cubicles take on a whole new meaning. The straights, once they are in a gay club can't resist a dabble. My knees are dirty every Saturday night. The wives and girlfriends all stand at the toilet entrance to see where their men are. When I walk past them from coming out of the toilet, I do think to myself if only they know how far their men can bend.

After another hour drinking and dancing, Halima says she is starving and wants some chips. So they all leave the club and pile into the chippy next door. Getting their food, they all sit down at a table. One of Andy's women friends comes over.

Karen
Are you Tracey? The bitch who has upset my Andy?

Tracey
Are you that slut who has made him lose everything?

Julie
Are you calling my girlfriend a slut?

Tracey
Yeah. I am.

Brenda
You know, you wait for a bus for hours then two come along at once.

Karen
What's that supposed to mean?

Brenda
I mean even a slut like you can get a free ride.

Karen
You see my friends over there, they don't think you bitches should be in here.

Lesley B
Is that right? Well that's funny, because I was thinking that slappers like you should be eating in a trough.

Julie slaps Lesley around the face. At the same time,. Tracey punches Karen in the face, making her fall back onto the table. Next minute, six women rush in and join the fighting.

Halima
That bitch has just knocked my chips out of my hand. (*She punches the woman in the face*) No-one touches my food!

Sandra

I feel like Calamity Jane. *(She starts singing wimp cracker way, wimp cracker way, then punches someone)*

Deb

(One of the woman kicks Deb between her legs. As she does so, Deb gets hold of her leg and swings her around. Deb let's go and the woman goes flying into the table) If I was a bloke that would have been a good move, but I'm a woman you thick bitch.

After twenty minutes of fighting with food and drink being thrown everywhere, the police rush in and arrest everyone. After another half a hour, Tracey's group finds themselves in one cell, and the others in the cell next door.

Brenda

It's like mother like son, me being banged up in here.

Sally

I'm supposed to be a manager.

Tracey

You should of thought about that when you were swinging that woman around by her hair.

Sally

You can talk, the way you punched that woman in the face. Are you married to Mike Tyson?

Deb

Just think ladies, if Halima had stuck to her diet and not wanted any chips we wouldn't be sitting here now. But it was a great night. A night spent as a family. *(Everyone nods their heads)*

At around eight o'clock in the morning, a police officer opens the cell doors.

Police officer
Good morning ladies, I trust we all slept well. Now there is a nice man at the front desk who has paid your fines. So you are free to go.

They all take it in turns to walk out of the police station. As they do so, they have to walk past Mr Thomas.

Deb
Thank you Mr Thomas.

Brenda
Thank you Mr Thomas. Your next breakfast is on me.

Sally
Thank you Mr Thomas. (Mr Thomas shakes his head)

Halima/Sandra
Thank you Mr Thomas.

As Tracey walks out of her cell, she sees Karen.

Karen
I'm sorry about last night. Too much to drink and a joint is not the best combination. We asked Andy to come back to ours, but he said no, and no man has ever said no to us before. He must really love you.

Tracey
He should have thought about that the first time round.

Karen
The amount of drink he had that night, there was no movement down below. We all deserve a second chance.

Tracey walks out of the police station.

Tracey

Thank you Mr Thomas.

Mr Thomas

There is someone to see you over there. I believe he has been there most of the night.

Tracey walks over to Andy.

Andy

I will do everything you want.

Tracey

It's for us.

Andy

Can I walk you to your gate?

Tracey

I have the mother of all hangovers, so I'm not really in a mood for talking. If you want to talk go and talk to a college. *(Tracey walks away)*

Lesley B walks out of the police station.

Mr Thomas

What have you go to say for yourself?

Lesley B

You were with another woman and you ask me what I've got to say for myself?

Mr Thomas

The other woman, as you call her, was my sister and the reason I had dinner with her was because I wanted to ask her opinion about something.

Lesley B
What would that be?

Mr Thomas
If she thought that it was too soon to get married again.

Lesley B
What did she say?

Mr Thomas
If you love the person enough, then time shouldn't be an issue. I told her that I love this woman with all my heart and that I want to be with her every day of my life.

Lesley B
Whoever this woman is, you better ask her to marry you then.

Mr Thomas
(Going down on one knee and holding up a diamond ring) Lesley Babbington, will you marry me?

Lesley B
(With tears in her eyes) Yes.

Tracey's Last Stand

Characters

Tracey, Lesley B, Sally, Halima, Sandra, Miss Spears, Mr Thomas, Brenda and Pop it in Pat.

Settings

Tracey's house, the factory.

Tracey's Last Stand

Tracey is sitting at her kitchen table, drinking tea and smoking a fag. Sally knocks on the door.

Tracey

Come in Sally love, the kettle has just boiled.

Sally

(Walking into the kitchen) Morning Tracey.

Tracey

Morning love. Pour yourself a cuppa.

Sally

I see the bills have arrived.

Tracey

(Looking at a bill) This can't be right. It is bloody August and the heating hasn't been on in months. By all means make a profit but don't get bloody greedy. I'll have to give them a ring.

Sally

Mine was the same. So I rang them up. They said that's what the reading said and because of it, they wanted me to up my monthly payments by twenty quid. I told them the summer months would put me back in credit again, so what is the point of paying an extra twenty quid, but she wouldn't have it.

Tracey

You know why that is don't you.

Sally

Why?

Tracey

The more profit you are in, the more interest they make. *(Tracey opens the phone bill)* Bloody hell, how has my phone bill got so high? I don't recognise half of these numbers. Who's number is 9265678? Who ever number it is, it is costing me over eight pounds in calls. Maybe Jay has got himself a new girlfriend. I will have to have words with that boy. I'll look at the rest when I get home. Come on, I don't want to be late on my last day.

Sally

(Picking up a letter off the table) Don't you want to look at this letter?

Tracey

It will just be someone wanting money.

Sally

What? With Nottingham University on the front of it?

Tracey

(Looking shocked, with her legs starting to shake, she sits down) Sally, this letter could change me forever.

Sally

(Passing Tracey the letter) Well, there's only one way to find out.

Tracey

(With her hands shaking) Sally I can't open it, you will have to do it.

Sally

Give it here. *(Sally opens the letter. There is a minute's silence as she reads what it says)*

Tracey

It's alright, you don't need to tell me. They don't want me.

Sally

(*Looking at Tracey*) Welcome to your new life.

Tracey

They haven't said yes?

Sally

That's what it says here.

Tracey

I can't believe it. A woman like me from a council estate, who has struggled all her life to survive, is going to university. (*She bursts out into tears*)

Sally

(*Giving Tracey a hug*) If there was ever a person who deserved it, it is you. All your hard work has paid off. Now, wipe your tears and let's get a move on, we are going to be late.

Both Tracey and Sally rush out of the door and walk down Mildenhall. As they walk past Mandy's house, Mandy comes out of the door with a bunch of flowers.

Mandy

These are for you, to wish you all the best for your new life.

Tracey

Thank you Mandy. How's baby Peggy?

Mandy

Just as loud as ever. She took her first steps yesterday. When she gets older, I hope she follows in your steps.

Tracey

Lets hope that her steps will be larger. (*She gives Mandy a hug*)

Sally

Come on girl, we are going to be late.

They both continue to walk down the hill and cross over Queens Bower Road. Five minutes later, they walk through the factory gates.

Tracey

Sally, do you mind if I sit with Bet for a minute?

Sally

Of course I don't, I'll clock you on.

Sally goes into the factory and Tracey goes to sit on the bench beside Bet's grave. She puts a flower that Mandy has given her next to Bet's headstone.

Tracey

(Talking out loud) Well girl, if there's one person I loathe to leave, it is you. I'm sure you will know by now that the little old me, Tracey Green from the council estate, has got into university. I still can't believe it. But I promise you Bet, now I've been given this amazing chance, I will work my ass off to succeed, and hope one day I can make you proud of me.

Lesley B comes over to Tracey.

Lesley B

I hear a congratulations is in order. Come here girl, let me give you a hug. *(They both have a long hug)* You will be pleased to know me and my future husband have set a date for our wedding. July the second, it's on a Saturday, so there is no excuse for you not to be there. Now, do you want your invitation to say Mrs Green, or shall I put Mrs Green plus one?

Tracey

Mrs Green plus one will be fine with me.

Lesley B

But we are not sure where to go on the honeymoon. He wants Cornwall, and I want two nights on the Orient Express and four nights in Venice.

Tracey

There's not much of a difference. I of course don't need to ask who is going to win?

Lesley B

You don't. But I want to see the tickets before I go up the aisle. *(They both laugh)*

Miss Spears

(Coming out of the factory) You might be engaged to the boss, but until you're married you will do as you're told and get some work done. So I suggest you pull your finger out and get on with some work. *(Lesley B walks back into the factory and Miss Spears sits next to Tracey on the bench. She takes Tracey's hand)*

Miss Spears

I would first like to congratulate you on getting into university.

Tracey

Thank you Miss Spears.

Miss Spears

Many years ago, I got into university on the same course that you are going to do. But the fool I was got myself pregnant by a guy who just walked away when I told him the situation. By the time I had an abortion, due to the fact there was no way I could look after a baby at the time, it was too late to go to university. So what I'm saying is go and succeed where I failed, and that way at least one of us will get to help the people who really need us.

Tracey

I will do my best.

Miss Spears

I'm sure you will. *(They both hug)* I know it's you're last day, but you are still getting paid to work. So let's be having you. But before you start, Mr Thomas wants a word with you in his office.

They both walk into the factory arm in arm. Tracey walks onto the shop floor, and as she does everyone stands up and applauds her. Next to her machine there are bunches of flowers and bottles of wine. She wave to everyone and blows them a kiss. She then walks into Mr Thomas' office.

Mr Thomas

Well Mrs Green, the day has finally come. Myself and everyone working here wish it hadn't, but we know you must leave in order to fulfil your dreams. As I've said before, you are always welcome to come back any time you need us. Once you come into this family you are always a part of it. Now, I want you to go and have your breakfast, then I have one job left for you to do and don't worry about this afternoon, you can go home at lunch time.

Tracey

That is so kind of you.

Mr Thomas

As I said, you are family. Now come and give me a hug. *(As they are hugging, Lesley B walks through the door)*

Lesley B

So this is what happens behind my back, you trollop, how could you?

Mr Thomas

Shut up woman. These might be of interest to you. *(He puts two holiday tickets onto his desk)*

Lesley B

You haven't booked the Orient Express and Venice have you?

Mr Thomas

Seeing as you haven't stopped going on about it for the last few weeks, I had to shut you up somehow.

Lesley B smothers Mr Thomas with kisses. Tracey, with a smile on her face, leaves Mr Thomas' office and goes into the canteen.

Brenda

Well here she is, Mrs University Green.

Tracey

Morning Brenda.

Brenda

Get yourself sat down, I'll bring it over.

Two minutes later, Brenda brings over a full English and a glass of bucks fizz.

Tracey

I'm going to miss your breakfasts.

Brenda

Just pop in any time. There will always be one waiting for you.

Tracey

Isn't it a bit early for champagne?

Brenda

It's never too early for someone as kind and special as you.

Tracey

You are a star.

Brenda

(Sitting next to Tracy) Have you spoken to Andy lately?

Tracey

Not since we were locked up.

Brenda

So you haven't heard?

Tracey

Heard what?

Brenda

He has left his wife and moved out into a one bedroom apartment.

Tracey

Has he?

Brenda

He has. He said he couldn't share a bed any more with a woman he felt nothing for. Many times he would wake up saying your names, having dreamt about you. As he said there is only one woman he wants to wake up to every morning. He has also been accepted into college to become an electrician.

Tracey

Lets hope he finishes the course.

Brenda

There is no question of that. He has too much to lose if he doesn't. Right, I must get on. Don't forget where we are.

Tracey

I won't. Thank you Bren. *(They both give each other a long hug)*

Tracey goes back downstairs to her machine. Miss Spears comes over to her.

Miss Spears
Mrs Green, Mr Thomas wants you to put some buttons and pockets onto this coat. It's a present for a member of his family. So please make sure you do a good job.

Tracey
I'll do my best.

Halima and Sandra walk over to Tracey.

Halima
Is that one of them designer coats? *(She feels the fabric)* That feels beautiful. Any woman would feel a million dollars wearing a coat like that.

Sandra
That would keep you warm on a cold winter's night.

Tracey
Well it's not going to be one of us who gets to wear it, not with what we get paid.

After a couple of hours, Tracey finishes the coat and walks over and hands it to Miss Spears.

Miss Spears
You have done a fantastic job on that. I'm sure Mr Thomas will be pleased. Right, Miss Babbington wants to see you in the union office.

Tracey walks over to the union office, where Lesley B is waiting for her.

Lesley B
It is my very sad duty to give you your p45 and a letter for you to

give the social security people. Is it too late to ask you to change your mind?

Tracey
There is part of me that so desperately wants to stay, but it is time for me to follow my dreams, because if I don't do it now I never will.

Lesley B
Don't forget you have a date on the second of July next year.

Tracey
I won't.

Lesley B
Right, I'll walk you out.

Tracey
(Walking onto the shop floor for the last time, Tracey stands still for a few minutes and remembers all the people who, past and present, she had worked alongside) Do you know Lesley, I'm taking with me a lot of wonderful memories. I was so blessed to work with some amazing people who have helped to make my many years here so happy.

Lesley B
That's the best present anyone could give to you.

Taking a last look at her machine, Tracey and Lesley climbs the stairs to the canteen. As Tracey opens the door, there is a big round of applause from all the workers.

Mr Thomas
(Standing in front of the canteen) Come and join me Mrs Green. *(Tracey stands next to Mr Thomas)* Although this is a sad day for the factory to lose one of its own, we know it is time for you to start your next journey. I hope it will give you as much happiness as this one has

done. Now we do have a couple of gifts for you. Mrs Macky?

Pat

Thank you Mr Thomas. As you know, we lost a dear and wonderful friend a few months ago. But fortunately we were able to bring her back home again where she belongs. So if it is alright with you Tracey, we would like to plant a tree next to Bet and call it Tracey's tree. As it grows, we all hope that your future will grow as well.

Tracey

I will be very proud and honoured to have a tree next to such a wonderful woman. *(Everyone claps)*

Mr Thomas

Miss Spears, I think you have something for Mrs Green

Miss Spears

Thank you Mr Thomas. Although it is a sad day for us, we all know and understand why you must leave us. Now, as a student who are famous for being skint, we didn't want you to go through the cold winters without a good coat to keep you warm. So when I asked you to finish off a coat to a high standard because it was for a member of Mr Thomas' family, that family member was you, Mrs Green. *(Miss Spears gives Tracey the coat)*

Tracey

(Giving Miss Spears a hug) Thank you Miss Spears, and thank you all for your love and generosity. A love that will stay with me always.

Mr Thomas

Finally, I want to give you a card that has been signed by everyone and a personal gift from myself to help you on your way to success.

Tracey

Thank you so much. *(They both hug as everyone claps)*

With tears in her eyes, Tracey makes her way to the door. She is seen hugging and kissing people as she goes. As she gets outside, everyone has followed her. They all stand by the factory entrance as she walks through the factory gates. Tracey turns one last time to wave to everybody, then she turns away, and walks towards home.

Printed in Great Britain
by Amazon